Deke Interrupted

Books by Ginna Gordon:

The Lavandula Series
  Book One: Looking for John Steinbeck
  Book Two: Deke Interrupted

The Honey Baby Darlin' Series
A serial memoir about cooking, love, & the love of cooking

  Book One – Bonnebrook Farm
  Book Two – The Gingerbread Farm

The Sunny Mae & Bird Read-Aloud Series
with illustrations by Dai Thomas

  Sunny Mae & Bird in Alaska

  Sunny Mae & Bird on Ice (2017)

First You Grow the Pumpkin:
100 Cool Things to Make and Preserve

The Marriage Tip Book:
Advice from the Wise Ones of the 2nd Grade
with Nan Heflin

A Simple Celebration:
The Nutritional Program from
the Chopra Center for Well Being
as Ginna Bell Bragg, with David Simon, MD
Foreword by Deepak Chopra (pub. by Random House)

Visit www.luckyvalleypress.com

Deke
Interrupted

Book Two in *The Lavandula Series*

based on the fictional journals
of Stefani Michel

Ginna Gordon

Cover Art and Tiny Paintings by
Dai Thomas

Lucky Valley Press
2017

Produced and Published in 2017
by Lucky Valley Press
Jacksonville, Oregon
www.luckyvalleypress.com

For Bonne "Babe" Conroy
1949-2016

Dear Babe,

I dedicate the entire *Lavandula Series*
about sisters and cousins to you.

My biggest fan since the crib,
you were the sister I never had.

As a cousin, a young cohort,
and an old pal, you were the best.

Thanks for telling me to
stop everything else and write.

With love,

Your favorite cousin

GB

Sweet Farm Cast of Characters
(showing their ages in 1963)

Author's Note

Sweet Farm is the stage on which our players play. It is a Carmel Valley, California lavender farm of some reknown. It is also the home of a revolving cast of characters all somehow related to the Wyman clan: farmers, artists, writers, musicians. They bond and clash in unusual ways as they create their lives one breath at a time.

The women are restless. The men are nervous. The girls are growing up in the 60s and they and their peers will become known as Baby Boomers, Flower Children, Hippies, Yuppies, the ME generation; they will be affected by the Vietnam War, Rock & Roll, revolutions from sexual to political, and dramatic social change. But mostly, they deal with their loves, children and homes as they relate to and are touched by those issues described above.

Deke Interrupted, Book Two in *The Lavandula Series*, begins with Stevie mapping her first sexual encounter and Jolene working out some guilt, while Tate and her mother get a big surprise.

There's more, of course. There's always more...

Deke Interrupted - Part 1

Excerpt from Stevie's Little Red Book

Maybe I'll Fall in Love
By Stefani Michel
15th birthday September 30 1963

We're growing up so fast
They said youth wouldn't last

They were right and I was wrong
And Tate can't sing this in a song
Life is moving right along
We're growing up so fast

It happened overnight
It gave me such a fright

My body curved
And then it swerved
And then, I lost my childhood nerve
It happened overnight

And it will happen to you
I tell you this is true

All of a sudden you are old
Your friends will tell you, This is gold!
But, it just leaves me in the cold
And it will happen to you

It makes me kind of blue
I tell you this is true

To think that I'm no longer young
My responsibility bell has rung
My childhood songs have all been sung
It makes me kind of blue

Maybe I'll fall in love
It's what they all speak of

My childhood gone but not forgotten
This grown-up thing can't be so rotten
Can something out of this be gotten?
Maybe I'll fall in love

Prologue

When Deke Harley met Fox Wyman in 1946, he was the proud owner of a blue Indian Chief motorcycle, an honorable discharge from the US Army declaring his military service obligation fulfilled thank you very much and a memory bank overflowing with sand, wind and sadness.

He lied to Fox back then when she asked him where his people were. Nova Scotia! He didn't even know where Nova Scotia was until later, when he secretly looked it up in the 1945 World Book Encyclopedia in Jock's den when Fox wasn't looking. *Good thing she didn't stick her foxy little snout into that one*, he thought at the time. His Oklahoma Panhandle, Cimarron County farm of dust and death story was a far cry from some lighthouse on the Atlantic.

When he left town, or drifted off, or maybe died four years later, in July, 1950, the day Fox became the self-proclaimed *Woman Deke Left*, she started looking for clues as to his whereabouts, and continued to do so long after the police gave up, because she knew he wasn't dead. She'd feel it in her bones, in her cells, on the tips of the red hairs on her arms, if he died. Part of her would be dead, like a dangling, useless limb, so she knew she'd feel that all the way through.

She couldn't find any Harleys in Nova Scotia. Not a one. After year 10, when she finally stopped counting the days, she gave up entirely. Because, who knew with a drifter? He could be anywhere by now. In whom or what could you trust in this world?

We come to love not by finding a perfect person
but by learning to see an imperfect person perfectly.
-Anonymous

NOVEMBER 1963
The Outrigger Polynesian Piano Bar
Cannery Row, Monterey
Sam's Perfect Stranger

This guy sat in a bar on Cannery Row in Monterey. It was safe there, no one to see him, no one knew him. He could play pool, he could have a beer. No one would care.

He'd been on the road for days and could use a little break from his perplexities. He felt like an escapee, sprung from jail by a triple layer chocolate cake with a file inside.

A young woman walked by the window. She looked in and saw him seated at the table. Their eyes locked for a split second. He saw her yesterday - she was beautiful, small, he guessed about 20, with rich dark hair in an unruly braid and smoky eyes, wearing a white t-shirt with rolled up sleeves and tucked into loose jeans.

The girl, for she was just a girl, walked past the Outrigger to the history-charged wooden stairs at Doc Ricketts' lab and sat on the bottom step. She stopped to exhale the breath she'd held since she first saw the man in the window. She knew he'd be there again today. She just knew.

She wet two fingers and slicked her hair at the temples, bit her lip for color, re-tucked the white t-shirt and examined her nails. The hem of her jeans unthreaded in nervous fingers.

Her eyes drifted around the scape of Cannery Row. The abandoned canneries and their new neighbors (so far: art gallery, bar/restaurant, dance studio and butterfly dealer, all very *not* abandoned) seemed a cultural collision. It made her think of something John Steinbeck said about fishing for tourists instead of pilchards - tourists being a species harder to wipe out.

She felt the salty sting of the ocean breeze. She saw that wharf cat, Pebbles, streak by with its gray tail up and hackles raised. This was daring, she knew, but what was life without a good dare? *Why should I wait for Prince Charming to come along and make promises? Why, indeed, should I wait for marriage, or, for that matter, someone to ask* me?

Half an Hour Later, in the Outrigger…

His cigarette burned down half an inch before he answered.

"I, ugh, I don't know what to say. I don't even know your name."

"My name is *Sam*," she said.

"Not your real name, I think."

"Real enough."

"Real enough for this?"

"Yes."

"You're determined."

"Yes."

"OK. So, let me get this straight. You want me, who you don't know from *Adam*…"

"*Adam!* That's your name! Now I know you."

"…who you don't know from *Adam*, or Mac, or the next guy over there at the bar, to take a room and have sex with you. In fact, you don't want to know my real name."

"Right. And yes."

"Why?"

"So I do it for the first time on my terms. I don't want to confuse it with love. I don't think it has anything, or much anyway, to do with love, and I want to know about it now. And, so I don't get pregnant. So no one in my life knows."

"Does anyone know?"

"Only one person. He's not telling."

"I have a feeling you're not really 20, either."

Silence.

"Is it clinical? You aren't looking for romance?"

"Not clinical. Beautiful."

"Oh, Lord. This conversation is out of hand already. Did you just walk in the door and proposition me?"

He looked around the room. Four single drinkers sat at the bar, involved in their own thoughts and, respectively: Pabst Blue Ribbon Beer, gin and tonic, Budweiser and one umbrella-trimmed Polynesian Dream Cocktail. The bartender wiped the back-bar mirror. No one listened or paid them any mind.

"Well, yes, I guess. Yes. And, before you ask, because I know you will, I am choosing you because you look nice and… right. My dad teaches me about really seeing people, and I believe you are a good person."

"Not all good."

"But, basically, good. You wouldn't hurt me."

He stared at her, his face un-masked, his eyes wide with a poorly hidden wonder. He didn't know whether to laugh or cry at this.

"No. I won't. I know that. Come hell or high water, I won't hurt you."

"Look, I just want to know. I want to know, before I embark on my adult life, that it is a beautiful thing. Is it? Can you say your sex life has been beautiful?"

Adam coughed. "Well, I have… well, yes. Partly. Yes." He squirmed on the red leather seat of the captain's chair.

"My grandfather says I read too many adult books, but the point is, I have read that women get hurt, or worse, raped, or have God-awful sex the first time and then hate it the rest of their lives. Would you wish that on me? I wouldn't wish it on my worst enemy."

Adam smiled. "No. I would not wish that on you. But I am not sure that this would be good for me."

"Oh. I hadn't thought of that. I thought any man would be jumping up and down to get an offer to deflower a cute virgin from the cute virgin herself."

Adam choked on the sip of beer sliding down the back of his throat. She watched him wipe the foamy spray off the table with his sleeve. Two men at the bar looked up.

"May I think about this, *Sam*? This is a big thing you're asking of a perfect stranger…"

"Not too long. I have time on Sunday. A long afternoon of time," she said meaningfully. "After that, well, I don't know. I have a… a complicated life. I don't know when I could manage it this perfectly again."

"Perfectly?"

"Yes. You. IT. The timing. It's perfect."

Stevie's Little Red Book

What would Sister William think about my plan? She will not know, as this little book is not for the probing eyes of nuns, even open-minded nuns willing to consider the follies of a precocious student.

Does that make me a liar? Ha. It's like keeping two sets of account books -- one for them, one for me: the juicy bits of my life, which are mine to keep, organized in my own fashion.

I'm only fifteen. How bad could it be, anyway?

November 1963
Sweet Farm, Carmel Valley
A Woman Comes to Call

Meanwhile, the mother of the incognito *Sam*, Rita Wyman Michel, about to close the Sweet Tea Room for the day, looked up as she locked the door. She saw a woman get out of a cab, slowly count out bills to pay the driver and, Rita thought, ask him to wait for her. The driver, a big jowly man with a small slouchy hat, pulled the cab over to the edge of the parking lot, facing Carmel Valley Road. He opened his window, turned off the engine, lit his pipe and settled in.

As the woman turned toward the Barn, she looked around Sweet Farm for signs of life: people working, lounging, moving about. She saw the east side of the Adobe House, the fields of neatly trimmed lavender beyond, and the Barn, where the front doors of Lavandula, Maria's studio, and the Sweet Tea Room were surrounded by Hostas and cineraria, fading now in fall. The stranger and Rita locked eyes. The woman squared her shoulders and moved forward. The gesture was familiar to Rita, but she couldn't place it.

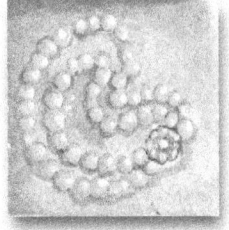

Rita walked down the path to the parking area, toward this lady who looked so out of place, with her pearls and softly pleated flowered dress and wide-brimmed straw hat. *Hasn't anyone told her it's November? And 1963?*

"Hello," said Rita, "May I help?" Her diminutive stature and breathy voice gave her away.

The woman said, "You must be Rita."

Whoop.

"Uhm, yes, that's me. And who are you?"

"Yes, well, that's it, isn't it? Who am I? Uhm, is your sister about? Fox, is it? I don't know her given name."

"Nora. But, Fox will do. Yes, she's here." Rita looked at her watch. "Over at the Adobe by now. The big house, there. It's past 5. Shall I get her? Do you have an appointment? It's late in the day for that, and she's probably…"

"Stay a moment, please. I should prepare you, and her. All of you. May we sit down somewhere? There, perhaps? On that bench?"

"Yes, OK. Or, better, come into the Tea Room. I was just closing, but the water is still warm. You look like you could use a cup of tea."

"Oh, yes. Wonderful. That would be lovely. Yes, a cup of tea."

Rita opened the door and ushered in her unexpected guest. She reached over to the water urn and felt its warmth, put some leaves in a pot, filled it with hot water and brought the teapot and two cups to the table where the woman sat on one of the lavender cushioned seats.

As she poured the tea, wary now, Rita said, "I still don't know your name."

With a sigh, the woman took off her hat, set it on the chair beside her, ran her fingers through her thinning grey/blonde hair, looked Rita square in the face and said, "My name is Rebecca Harris. Rebecca Harris… Harley."

Rita stopped, mid-pour. She sat down and looked at the woman in the softly pleated flowered dress.

"Oh my, my, my, my."

Fox. Fox. Where is Fox, anyway?

Rita Wyman Michel and Rebecca Harris Harley sat in silence while Rita absorbed this information. No matter who this woman was or what she had to say, a breath held for thirteen years was about to exhale all over Mid Valley.

Ho boy.

> *When two people meet, each one is changed by the other*
> *so you've got two new people.*
> -John Steinbeck

November 1963
Sweet Farm, Carmel Valley
Salinas
Stevie and Farley on the Phone

She called herself *Sam* (as it happens, her initials), and she was not 20, but a mere 15. She'd read recently and completely believed that a girl's first notion of sex will follow her the rest of her life, and she wanted to be in charge of it, to know what she was doing. Her friend, Carol, was unpleasantly deflowered by a untrustworthy de-frocked priest, and she, Carol, will carry this burdensome sack on her shoulders forever. It was not in the least beautiful.

No. Not for our *Sam*. She had in mind a sweet encounter, with someone who could awaken her to the joys of sex without hurting her. If she went into it knowing the score, even with a stranger, isn't that OK? Especially with a stranger! No one need know but her. And him. Whoever he would be.

Finally, after months of pondering this idea and keeping her eye out all over Monterey County for the Perfect Stranger, she saw him, and she knew.

"What's wrong with *me*?" Farley asked with a pubescent squeak during their late night phone call the night before, when she spilled her latest plan into the ear of her best boy-pal via her new red princess phone. They were each under the covers in bed, he in Salinas on his parents' Molera Road hill, she in Carmel Valley, tucked into the Chapel House, her family's tiny cottage at Sweet Farm. "I'm safe, you know me, I would never hurt you, and you know I love you."

"Oh, but, that's just it, Farls. You do know me. And, we aren't like that."

"Speak for yourself."

Stevie ignored this. "I need someone, hmmm, outside our circle. I am choosing a complete stranger. Then, there will be no complications."

"Well, fat chance of that."

"Shut up. It'll be fine. I am fine. My eyes are open. It's only for about an hour, maybe two."

"What! You'll be fine in a downtown Monterey motel room with a stranger? You're jailbait! Your parents would flip!"

"That's why we're not telling them. Besides, first you think it should be you, now I'm jailbait! I'll have a room with a phone. I'll call you if there is trouble. But there won't be. I'm choosing well."

"Ha. Who else knows about this? And, why did you tell me?" asked Farley, worry in his beautiful, soulful brown eyes. With his horn-rimmed glasses, he looked like Gregory Peck. Without glasses, lying under the covers in plaid flannel pajamas, using his big sister's pink push-button phone with extra long coiled pink cord, he looked like a very young boy.

Farley had his Gregory Peck eyes on his best friend. He planned to marry her one day.

He never told Stevie this. She would be the last to know, but his parents saw, and her cousins knew, and Stevie's parents, Fáno and Rita, oblivious as they usually were, suspected, but they knew Stevie loved Farley as a friend, no more.

"Well, no one but you knows. I'll tell Tate after. She'd only worry, and maybe be ticked off. Well, she'll be ticked, sure enough." Our little she-goat was on this, and we know what that means. "And, I am telling you because I trust you. I need an ally. It has to be you."

"Rita and Fáno will have my hide if they ever find out I knew about this."

"They will not find out unless you tell them." In the dark and under the covers, she gave the red phone the look she'd inherited from her grandmother, Maria. The Gimlet. It was a beady look, intense and hard. Her jaw was set. Actually, she did resemble a goat. On Molera Road at the other end of the phone connection, Farley felt her stubborn goatness.

"They will not find out," Stevie repeated.

NOVEMBER 1963

Sweet Farm, Carmel Valley
The Visit of Visits Part 1

Rita ran to the back of the Barn, gathered up the mystified but unquestioning Fáno, pulled him along by the hand and braced herself as she ascended the steps to the Adobe and opened the sliding door into the Middle, the family gathering place, the great room. *What luck the girls aren't here*, Rita thought. *This is crazy. Right now, Fox. What to say? What to say?*

"Hey, Rita, Fáno, you're finally here. I was about to come and get you," Fox said from the kitchen counter. Fox didn't notice her sister's eyes widen in horror. "I have an idea for the Tea Room, if you're willing to hear it. This wine is good - would you like a glass, Fáno? I've got…"

"Fox.. I…"

"… a little of this smelly Camembert, and…"

Jock walked in from his little den and said to Rita, "Hello, little darlin'. What's that cab doing out there? Did I see someone go into the Tea Room with you?"

And then, Mama Maria stepped in from their bedroom.

"Ok." Rita put up her hand to get their attention, like a white-gloved traffic cop. If she owned a whistle, she would bleat an S.T.O.P! "You're all here. I need you to please just stop. Stop everything. Sit down. Anywhere. Just sit."

Fox looked up from licking her fingers, blissfully ignorant for just one more moment. Maria observed her oldest daughter, the little Rita, whom she adored and who she felt was a bit flighty, successful Tea Room or no. Still, Maria dutifully sat by the fire and picked up her knitting, counted a few stitches to remind herself where she was in the project, and started clicking her wooden needles. Her Inner French Critic sighed.

Fáno, still dressed in loose denim work overalls and flowered shirt, kerchief tied around his dark curly hair, sat by the hearth, where he and Rita mostly listened to conversations, but she obviously had something on her mind, so he waited. The calico cat, Mesmer, jumped into his lap for a canoodle.

Jock mixed himself a drink. "Pour me something, Poppy. Anything. I don't care."

This got their attention. Rita was not a drinker.

Jock handed her a glass of sherry and leaned against the piano.

Fox scraped the cheese off her fingers with a little knife and then her tongue and smiled at her sister.

"What's up, honey? You look all distressed. What is it?"

"Sit, Fox. Now. Obey me like a good puppy. Sit down right over here, in this chair by me. Please. Just do as I say."

Fox wiped her hands on a napkin and went over to her sister. She sat. And then looked worried. Juana looked up from chopping carrots at the kitchen counter. She and Rita exchanged a glance. Juana knew it was big. She knew her friend Rita almost better than anyone.

Rita took in her audience with her eyes. She looked at Fáno for strength. She had about two seconds to reassemble her nerves before giving the folks the news of the decade; of the millennium, maybe. Of ever.

She took a sip of sherry and then sipped again. She set the glass down on a little table and held onto the chair in which her youngest sister sat at alert. Oh, serious ripples in the collective blanket were coming.

"I... oh. Fox, there is something I have to tell you and... and I need you to just listen..."

"Tate! What's happened to Tate? Oh, God, no!" Fox made to get out of the chair, but Rita held her back.

"No. Tate's fine. No. Stop. It's not really bad, what I have to say. But it will shock you just the same. Just sit there."

So she did. As did everyone else, now expectant.

Rita tried again.

"Fox, I don't know how to say this except just say it. There is no reason or any way to put it off. This is about Deke." She let that sink in. Every last eye in the place was riveted on Rita. "His mother is here."

"What? Deke's mother? I thought she was dead? What?"

"It's Deke's mother all right. Don't ask me how I know."

Rita looked around the room again, making sure they all knew she was dead serious. Fáno dumped the cat, who shook her booty at the whole business and left the room in a huff, while Fáno came to Rita's side.

Rita sat on the arm of the chair and took her sister's hand. "Honey, it's true. She is here. She is here, in the Tea Room, sitting at a table, drinking tea and nibbling a biscuit like a faded southern belle right out of a romance novel. She is here, in the flesh, with a straw hat and pearls and white gloves and a letter and…"

Rita took a breath, and plunged into deep water.

"…and I need to tell you something else."

Fox was staring at her, transfixed. Rita took another long pause.

"I don't know the details, but…" and here she thought long and hard before she let this giant tiger out of its cage, "Deke is alive."

Fox combined a little squeak and a faint and slumped against her sister. Her face turned white and her eyes fluttered. Rita could feel Fox's shallow breaths against her bare neck, where the younger sister pressed in against the older.

Everyone was up now, moving toward the sisters, but Fáno put up his hand. "Shhhh," he whispered. "Geeve them space. Sh-sh-sh. Eet'z OK. Eet'z OK." Poppy held Maria. Rita held Fox. Juana slipped out the back door to find Felix, to get him in here lickety-split.

The room was hushed, like that feeling inside a church just before the Mass begins. Fox squeezed her sister's hand until it turned blue.

Lady Charlotte's Flat, London
The Key

Jolene still carried the secret about her father's last night on earth in an imaginary box. Around this imaginary box were layers of imaginary quilts and spider webs and rolls of imaginary sheet music, all felted together and shrunk around it. She hid it well, no one suspected. Jolene had become a very good hider.

Jolene thought perhaps the key hanging on a chain around her mother's neck was the key to that box. The key was all Chuck left to Nana, besides Jolene herself. She imagined locking the imaginary box and layering stuff all over it. She planned to snatch the stupid real

key off her mother's real neck and throw it all off Bixby Bridge, the very scene of Chuck's demise. All people would see is Jolene throwing nothing into the water. It was the throwing that counted.

In the three years since her father, Charles Huffington, crashed his Volkswagen off the cliff by Bixby Bridge, Jolene hadn't found the courage to go near it. It chilled her to think that her dad loved a bridge in Carmel Valley and died under one in Big Sur.

The longer things went on, the further she got from revealing the truth about Chuck's last words. *Don't tell, Jo.*

It just seemed useless - what would it prove? That he *was* crazy? That she killed him by her silence? By her acquiescence to his terms of secrecy?

How would it feel to stand on Bixby Bridge? *If I ever want to go to Big Sur again, I'd better make peace with that bridge.*

And, as to her mother's state of affairs, she'd known about William for ages, even before her father died. She knew what anxious, whispered phone calls in the wee hours were all about. She knew the signs of extramarital activities: mussed hair, phone hang-ups, guilty-as-all-get-out looks in her guilty eyes. Sure, she knew.

Jolene wished her mother would just get on with it. *Daddy's dead, Mum, and you didn't care, anyway. Go be with your fusspot, William.* But she didn't say it. She wasn't cruel.

And the key thing! Jolene was pretty certain that the key was just a fantasy of Chuck's, a romantic gesture at the last minute. *Oh, Nana, I love you so much I left you the key to my heart!* Or some such. It's probably a key he found in a junkyard - or under that Schulte Road Bridge! It's certainly a gesture his alter ego, the Super Conductor, would think of.

Jolene tried to stay on the subject at hand with her mother.

"Mum. What could the key possibly open? You've checked every bank in England and every door and window and box and drawer in every manor and estate Daddy ever entered; every dressing room of every venue, every closet in London. I know you even went in disguise and checked behind the bar in that London Hotel Lounge, scene of the final botch. I don't even know if I think that's funny. What? What next?"

"I don't know, Jolene," Nana said, fingering the key. "All I can tell you is that this is what he left me. He left it with no note. He left a key. What am I supposed to do? Hang it on this chain around my neck forever, like a charm? A promise ring? No. It has a purpose. And I'll find it. I don't even care what the purpose is anymore. I need to find it. I don't think I can get on with the rest of my life until I find it."

Back to Sweet Farm
Inside Fox's Head

Fox thought she might be dying or having a heart attack. Her breathing was so quick and shallow she began to hyperventilate. She saw stars and flickery sparkly shapes like a kaleidoscope of electric snowflakes in the backs of her eyes, and her body began to sway. She flicked her eyes open and saw the fine hairs on her sister's neck, moving up and down with Rita's calm breath. Up and down. Up and down. Fox focused her attention on the hairs. Up and down. She thought if she kept her eyes open the room would stop spinning and she'd be back at the counter with Camembert on her fingers and this last ten minutes would be just another daydream, another wayward thought of the errant Deke.

Meanwhile, her arms wrapped around her sister like tape on a package, and her face pressed close to Rita's skin.

Fox saw the last thirteen years like a movie, a documentary flashing before her open eyes, every little detail of loss and loneliness, pain and anger and fear and unshed tear. Every time she went to bed and got up without him. Every time she looked at the one remaining photo of Deke tucked away from prying eyes in the drawer of her bedside table (since, in a fit of pique more than a decade ago, she'd torched the rest).

She thought of Deke the last time she'd seen him, at the Rodeo grounds in Salinas that Saturday morning in July, 1950. She groaned when she envisioned that mop of blonde hair and his Warren Beatty teeth. He winked at her, like always. He'd wink at her and say, "See ya, Foxie." Like he did that day.

She let herself think, just this once, of that Saturday morning of the Rodeo, their last intimate moments together before Fox's world collapsed in on her like a circus tent. They'd been snuggling under the covers, "spooning," Deke called it. He curved his body entirely around hers. He whispered nonsensical things in her ear: Juicy Fruit. Bumble Shoot. Hardly Mute. Happy Toot. Mistletoe. Grandpa Joe. His arms wrapped around her torso and cupped her tiny breasts. His legs entwined with hers. She could feel every bit of him, from her head down to her toes, skin to skin.

She was facing the edge of the bed, giggling with happiness, enjoying the sensation of a full body press. Deke was snuffling and blowing in her ear and no longer even pretending to say words in any language but the whispered ones of lovers. Fox heard a little noise and opened her eyes to find the 2½ year old Tate standing by the side of the bed, looking intently at her mother's smiling face poking up out of the covers.

"Wat doin'?"

Fox remembered how they'd pulled Tate onto the quilts with them and laughed and laughed and Tate laughed too. They got up and dressed and made scrambled eggs which they folded into warm corn tortillas and parchment and went off to the Rodeo with breakfasts in hands. Deke dropped Fox and Tate off at the entrance gate and said he had a couple of errands to run. "See ya, Foxie." He never came back.

Fox started to laugh right there in the Middle of the Adobe, sitting in a chair with her face pressed to her sister's neck. At first it was small, under her breath, a kind of desperate giggle. Then it got bigger and scarier, like a snowball careening down a hill toward her at high speed with a cold wind, and she began to shake. Then, frenzied laughing took over completely and she felt like a very hysterical manic crazy person. She laughed and laughed until her parents and her sister and Fáno and Juana and Felix got worried and considered first aid. Then, she looked up into their concerned faces, and cried.

MAY 1961
Flashback
Primrose Summit, London

Nana and William sat side by side on the grassy knoll of Primrose Summit, looking out along the London skyline, glowing and pulsing like footlights on the stage of the gods. A full moon in the dark sky on a clear night brought Nana and William out of his apartment and onto their bikes at midnight. The twosome agreed they were in the dark in the park on a lark.

Their bikes were in the grass behind them. Nana and William leaned into each other, touching from shoulder to waist. The picnic: a half bottle of vintage port, two small wedges of cheese (one blue, one cheddar), a small slab of butter, 4 cold sausages, a small loaf of crusty French bread and two Cadbury Crème Eggs wrapped in colored foil, nested in its little basket at the edge of the red and green Cameron Tartan blanket.

Nana arrived that morning on an overnight flight from the States. It was Spring, 1961, and Nana, a widow of six months, appeared on William's doorstep unannounced at approximately 4pm, with the little picnic basket in her left hand and two dozen yellow roses tucked under her left arm. She set down the overnight bag she'd carried in her right hand all the way from the airport and throughout her picnic errands, and rang the doorbell.

Nana was pretty sure Will did not have a singing engagement that night and would be awake and perhaps practicing at this hour. But, she did not hear his clear tenor voice spilling its lyric wonder out the window, and there was no sound of the piano, either. *Oops*, she thought. *Perhaps I should have called. He certainly wasn't expecting me.*

Just then she heard his distinctive shuffle across the hardwood floor of the hallway. *Ah. He's wearing his fuzzy slippers*, she thought, *and probably an old pair of corduroy pants, hmmm, dark green, and… let's see, the black smoking jacket, silk and quilted on the outside, soft flannel on the inside.*

Nana was nervous. She had been silent these six months, needing the time on her own. It's not every day a woman becomes a widow when her half-estranged husband crashes their VW Bug off the cliff at Bixby Bridge in Big Sur and lands on the sand.

And, even though she was no longer in love with Chuck when this happened, it happened on her watch, and in her mind, she had failed. She had failed Chuck, and Jolene, and perhaps even William. She couldn't save her marriage, she couldn't keep Jolene's father from killing himself, and even if it was not suicide (the jury inside her head was definitely still out on that) he was drunk on wheels, and she felt that was her fault too, because she couldn't love him enough or make him love her enough to keep him sober. All that prattle from Lady Charlotte about family craziness notwithstanding, she could have tried harder. Charlotte's was a weak explanation.

It took courage for Nana to be standing here on William's doorstep, and it was beginning to fail as he opened the door. She remembered the phone call in which she'd asked him to be patient, the several attempts he made at contact before he realized she was serious, and the lonely months at Sweet Farm, grieving the loss of someone she didn't love while longing for someone she shouldn't have been loving.

The complications of it all were swirling in her head when William's sweet face appeared in the open door. Oh, yes, indeed: smoking jacket, corduroy pants.

He looked at her in silence for a moment, which was just enough time to trigger Nana's reflex to bolt (runs in the family), when he laughed and said, "Yellow roses?" as he picked up her bag, put his other hand on her arm and pulled her in.

November 1963
Sweet Farm, Carmel Valley
Fox Gets A Message

Dear Fox,

It is really me. I am nearby and hope to see you. I will explain everything. Please forgive me, but you will understand, I think, if you let me come.

Please, Foxie, tell me I can come to you.

Deke Harley

Fox sat in her chair in the Middle, immobilized. Ordinarily, this room was womb-ish: close to her parents' warm sanctuary, a lovely fire, all the family gathered, warm food and aromas of things to come. Now, people were murmuring around her, but she didn't notice. She didn't hold the note, she squeezed it between her fingers. Like Deke was in there. She held it like it would poof away, like smoke. Like Deke.

Her family members watched her covertly as they welcomed the surprise Mother of Deke into the fold. As for Fox, she hadn't once looked at the woman after Rebecca handed her the note. There was no preamble. No speech. No warm hug or exclamation. The Mother of Deke floated into the room like a ghost: ethereal, fragile. Her voice was a whisper. "This is for you, Fox."

Thirteen years! Thirteen years! And he sends his mother? Dammit!

Rebecca hesitated when Jock finally asked for some details. "I am so sorry," she said in her soft Maryland drawl. "I have promised the boy to let him tell his own story. I know what you're thinking, Fox." She set the tea down and turned to the mother of her granddaughter. "I know you must think him a coward, for being away so long, and for not coming himself. But, we agreed that I could perhaps soften the shock of it, pave the way a bit. I cannot say more, Fox, because I promised the boy."

"That boy is 40 years old, Mrs. Harley." These were the first and only words Fox spoke, and they were barely above a squeak.

"Yes." Rebecca pulled the little hearth stool up close to the chair in which Fox sat crunching the note in one hand and gripping the arm of the chair with the other. Rebecca adjusted the fall of her flowered skirt and put her hand gently on Fox's knee.

"Fox, I don't know you, but my son loves you and you have a daughter whom I'd like to know. All I can say is that I stand behind Michael in this, because he has been sorely hurt, and when you hear what he has to say to you, why, I hope you will have it in your heart to forgive his apparent disinterest in your lives. He has been compromised and through many bad times. But, it is not my tale to tell."

Rebecca stood up and put on her straw hat.

"We are staying at the Monterey Downtown Hotel. I shall return to him now and give him your answer. Will you see him tomorrow, Fox?"

November 1963
Sweet Farm, Carmel Valley
Fox Gets Ready

Fox and Rita stayed in the Adobe that night, in Nana's room in the four-poster bed of their childhood. They wanted to be near Poppy and Maria. Rita and Fox didn't talk much, but they didn't sleep, either.

What words?

They had no information about Deke except that he was alive and he was coming over tomorrow at 10am. And something more, something… off.

Well, it was all off.

Fox, in a state of red-headed shock, sat rigid on the bed at 5 on Saturday morning, her knees bent, her arms wrapped in a grip around her legs. Rita was dozing, snuffling in half-sleep with her hand on Fox's arm.

But there had been no sleep for Fox. She thought it a bit cruel of the Harleys to keep her waiting, but perhaps it was best. It gave her time to let it sink in.

Deke was alive. Deke was Michael Harris Harley. Deke… here.

Deke. Is here.

NOVEMBER 1963
Cannery Row, Monterey
Adam

A*dam* left the bar and found the path down to the ocean's edge. He sat on a rock, felt the sea breeze, noticed sea gulls swooping overhead, tourists exploring, boats bobbing in the bay.

I'd like to be on one of those boats right now, he thought. *Just sail away, on and forever. On and forever. Being fenced in isn't good for a man.*

I have to say no to the girl. Sam. She must be underage, and I'm out of practice, anyway. She's probably got some big burly brother somewhere just itching to protect her virtue. I'd be shot. That'd be no good.

Why couldn't I just flat out say no to her back there? I handled that all wrong. What was I… embarrassed? Chicken? Worried? Hard to reject her, let her down. But, really.

Do girls do that nowadays? Come right out and ask for it?

Stevie's Little Red Book

Jolene, in London now at Woolsley, living in a "house" with 10 other girls in the prep school, doesn't want to lose touch with her Englishness. Perhaps she thought we'd turn her into a heathen. Ruin her English.

Perhaps it's the nuns. I can only imagine a girls' school on a huge beautiful campus near a big metropolitan city taught by regular people in street clothes living real lives, not Dominicans in flowing habits cloistered in hallowed halls dedicated to the Virgin Mary.

Tate is not so affected by Jolene's departure, but I feel it keenly. Jolene and I were in the same class and, even in mourning, she gave school her best shot and was a crackerjack good friend and student. I felt better in her presence, not so odd, and I liked school more: I was associated with the fabulously beautiful and exotic flaming redheaded, Brit-accented English girl, Jolene Huffington.

1961
Flashback, continued
William Cameron

Will Cameron: the ultimate professional, the show-up guy, the reliable one who could take over a role at the last minute, get the gal ("Lyric tenors always get the gal," he said with a wink), and gave his all to every role, big and small. Lovely William, trained by his friend and mentor, Dame Alicia Markova, to carry himself like a dancer and to maintain that elegant presence on the stage for which he was famous. She also poised him on the ballet bar a few times, but his body type was more suited to less active sports, like drinking tea and reading.

At the height of his career, William's schedule was tight and focused: his calendar kept by his agent in London, his travel arrangements made by a service. His Spanish maid, Olivia Sanx, showed up twice a week to keep up with William's somewhat haphazard housekeeping.

William Cameron was a free spirit. At home, he tended to shuffle in his slippers. He had a slight slump. He lounged in pajamas and smoked the occasional pipe with sweet smelling bohemian tobaccos. The newspapers, for he perused several each day, piled up in corners, reduced by Olivia each Friday.

His furniture captured the past in old polished wood and ancient red velvet. His mother's tassel collection hung on doorknobs and curtain hooks, the drawer knobs of antique sideboards and the arms of overstuffed chairs.

William's 75-year-old mother, Beva Green Cameron Slade, known as the Old Artist, lived up the front stairs in a large apartment, where Olivia also attended to household chores and took care of Beva's daily needs when William wasn't able.

A grand piano dominated William's front room, string instruments filled the walls, and stray sheets of music flew in the breeze from the open window and onto the threadbare Turkish carpet, thinned by the tread of genteel shoes over years of living and playing in this room.

It was a dusting challenge, but Olivia enjoyed her job. Why wouldn't she? She 1) took home for dinner portions of any food she made in William's kitchen for him and his mother, 2) heard opera arias and German Lieder all day at least twice a week when he was in town, sung like an angel descended from Heaven for her little Spanish ears alone, 3) loved the Old Artist, and 4) was paid regularly, also by the agent, so a pause never occurred due to William's casual attendance to details.

William was more adventurous and less of a fusspot than Jolene thought. He was just shy and rather ego-less. Jolene's lens, zoomed in on her own teenaged life in Technicolor as it was, did not include the opera world in its scope, so she had no idea her mother's half-secret boyfriend was a hot British ticket.

It was not lost on Nana that she loved another British musician. But that is where the similarities between Charles Huffington and William Cameron end.

November 1963
Carmel Valley Village
Tate and Stevie Go to a Party

By the time she and Tate arrived at Sadie's on Esquiline Drive in the Village for the birthday slumber party on Friday night, Stevie's insides had turned inside out. She was sure her heart was on her sleeve.

She'd lied to herself about all the logical reasons for choosing *Adam*: she was stirred up to beat the band! *He's so beautiful*, she thought. *Older than I imagined, but really gorgeous. That hair! And, he really is nice.* All her calm left her. She could think about nothing but *Adam*.

And she couldn't tell anyone. No time or privacy to call Farley, and he'd have fits, anyway. She'd best leave it alone for the moment.

> *Madam I'm Adam*
> *Adam I'm Sam*
> *Where will this take me?*
> *Fool that I am*
>
> *Is this love?*
> *But who am I kidding?*
> *Love doesn't come along*
> *At one's bidding*

Although it isn't love
That I'm seeking,
I stink of love
I'm practically wreaking

Does no one else notice this
but me?
Isn't it obvious?
Can't they see?

What's this Perfect Stranger
doing to me?

Sweet Farm, Carmel Valley
The Visit of Visits, Part 2

The same yellow cab with the big man at the wheel pulled into the Sweet Farm driveway in front of the Barn at 10:15 on Saturday morning. This time, the driver did not turn the car around and discreetly park under the trees, but just turned off the engine and lit his pipe, as if about to watch a play. Perhaps this was his story to take home to Mabel, his wife, who waited patiently each night with a cold beer to hear about his day. Or perhaps he was just trying to figure it out. It was a good puzzle.

The two people in the cab's back seat sat very still, slowly breathing in and out. They did not notice the driver. They did not look at the house, or the Barn or the trees outlined along the top of Saddle Mountain. They didn't even look at each other. Their eyes were focused inward, seeing where their courage lay, that which started them on this quest three years earlier, when Deke experienced his epiphany about his life: when he remembered to think about Fox. His daughter. Their tribe.

Fox, sleep-deprived and bleary-eyed, sat in the chair by the fire, wrapped in a quilt for security more than warmth. It was the Quilt of Many Colors from her bed, made by Mama Maria in 1945 from Fox's childhood clothes, cut in eight-inch mostly cotton squares, pressed and stacked neatly in the closet until there were enough squares to cover a double bed. It covered Fox now in her distress, but it was not enough.

Fox had wandered near and far in the night, wide awake: into this sweet memory (the two of them on his cot in the Bunk House) and that bitter thought (*Dammit!*), from this blissful moment to those pesky and painful feelings deep in her female core that had called to Deke over thirteen long lonely years.

"Where the GD Sam Hill have you been?" she wanted to scream. Wanted to yell. Wanted to perforate the sky with sharp pointy words! "Why? Why this? Why now? Dammit!"

She was used to the lonely life, settled into it, numbed to stillness. What could come of this?

And, yet. Isn't this what she had waited for all this time? For him to just come home?

And, what of Tate? she thought. *She'll arrive this afternoon to… what?*

Earlier that morning, Maria asked Sadie's parents to keep the two girls occupied for a few extra hours, which gave this situation time to… *expand into a full-blooming predicament! Tate. Oh my Lord in heaven.*

Was he still boyish? Beautiful? And how would his eyes see her? She looked in the hand mirror too many times and then threw it on the floor in disgust. *I am what I am. Dammit! How can this be happening?*

When Rita awoke next to Fox, she was stiff from sleeping wrapped half around her sister. Waking up, Rita thought, *This is something! Really something! In a way, I can hardly wait to see!*

"What will you wear?" Rita asked her sister, unaware that Fox had detached herself from Rita's arms hours ago, took the hottest bath on the planet, which Rita slept right through, and changed her clothes four times before deciding on the jeans she'd worn yesterday, a half-clean white cotton sweater miles too big and two pairs of socks. She then got back on the bed and snuggled up to her sister, hoping Rita's calm little aura would shed some light on her own person and make this day OK.

It didn't. Oh, the light was shed all over Fox, Rita could do that, but Fox knew this day was hers to face, and she was gathering her wits.

"I am wearing it."

"Oh," said Rita. "Really?" Her brow furrowed.

"C'mon, Rita, I am not dolling myself up for Deke Harley, who's been gone thirteen years and is too chicken to come himself but sends his poor worn-out mother! What do you think I should wear? A dress and a parasol? Nope. I'm fine."

"Well, comb your hair, anyway. You look like Lucille Ball."

1961

London
Flashback, continued
Nana and William

Once inside the door of William's apartment, Nana and Will merged into a long embrace. He held her close but gently, as if she might break. *God knows*, he thought, *the girl's been through hell.*

He was surprised to see her this day, but expected her sooner or later because he hadn't felt any threads break between them. They were still attached, and here she was.

Nana's tall elegant body loomed over William, especially at home, where she insisted he was three inches shorter than on stage. How did he do that?

The hug found Nana's lips grazing the top of William's round head full of soft brown curls, and his lips were close to her bosom. Once when she laughed at them upon seeing their side-by-side reflection in a mirror, he said, "You have a very nice bosom and I don't mind it one bit and besides, when we are horizontal, it doesn't matter who is taller."

He let her go, took the picnic basket and said, "Come..." and held her hand. Somehow the flowers found their way into a vase and the picnic was set aside. Nana and William whirled down the hall to his unkempt bedroom, where books and papers piled helter-skelter and, under a bright window, a collection of unmatched socks lined up like wallflowers awaiting dance partners.

Hours later, after murmured conversation and tender embraces and perhaps a wink or two of sleep, they made their way back to the kitchen. William asked again, "Yellow roses?"

Nana sat down at the counter to watch Will make coffee. She was wrapped in his forest green terrycloth dressing gown, too big and too short at once. She sighed, half frowned-half smiled and said, "Yellow roses are for new beginnings. They mean, 'Remember me?'"

"You're coming home, then? This isn't just a visit?" Will, holding the coffee press, turned around to face her.

Sadie's House
Esquiline Drive, Carmel Valley Village
Stevie tries to stay on track

Tate, designated party singer and leader of musicals, set up the portable tape recorder with seven-inch reels in Sadie's big bedroom and plugged it into the wall and microphone.

Sadie found a stool for Tate and came up with her father's beat-up guitar, sadly out of tune but tunable. Tate was game. Heck, she'd learned about the beat with a wooden spoon and the bottom of a stockpot. She could bang on this ol' thing.

The bedrolls were laid out around the room, the blankies were in place, the pizza and salad gobbled up indelicately. Six girls gathered and giggled, something for which Stevie had little patience in general.

What dolts, she thought uncharitably. *Do they ever talk about anything except lipstick and boys?*

I've got a man on my mind!

And, oh, what a man! Stevie saw his beautiful face in the pizza, the tile, the crack in the ceiling, the Coke bottle. She went over and over their half hour conversation. She thought of the last words he spoke to her.

"You'll know."

What had she said to him? "How will I know if you're going to meet me on Sunday?" And then he spoke quietly, got up slowly and walked away, leaving some dollar bills on the bar for his beer, her lemonade and a generous tip.

When *Adam* turned the corner and disappeared, Stevie's bravado deflated. She left the Outrigger in a hurry and walked a few blocks of the Row to calm her fluttering heart before going up the hill to Wave Street, where she caught the bus to Carmel.

On the way to meet Tate, *Adam* consumed her: the way his fingers played with the cocktail napkin, curling the edges like a hanky with a hand-rolled hem and then flattening it out and folding it into little origami patterns; the way the light from the window played on the pale blue shadows under his eyes; his combination of amusement and shock at her… proposal. Was love like this, she wondered? Because, if so, she'd already ruined her perfect plan by falling in love with the Perfect Stranger. This was not the idea.

Or was she just attracted to him, animal magnetism and all that? If this was so, then OK. It just adds to the raw beauty of the moment.

Whichever the case, her body vibrated with anticipation. Her heart beat at the speed of light. Her chest heaved, breathing in his remembered scent.

Crikey, she thought, quoting her English cousin. *It's like someone's laid an enchantment on me.*

Tate poked her side. "Hey!" she whispered.

"Ow. What?"

"Are you even in there? Paying attention? I asked if you wanted to sing a duet with me to start this hootenanny or whatever off on the right foot. I don't know. *500 Miles? If I had a Hammer?* Something Peter, Paul and Mary, easy to sing along."

"Sure. OK. Whatever."

"Don't sound so excited."

"I'm sorry. I'm… I'm with Patricia."

Ah! Their code for *Stevie's having a creative surge.* Clever of Stevie, in the moment. When Patricia, her muse, whispered stories in her ear, Stevie listened. Patricia claimed to be a French ancestor and indeed, her accent often made Stevie think of her grandmother, Mama Maria. She resembled Dorothy Malone, with deep eyelids and extra long lashes that created wind when she blinked. Patricia stood no taller than six inches and often perched on Stevie's right shoulder, mostly sitting with her legs crossed, smoking. Patricia was 1920s thin, with long, straight bangs and a lovely bob, expertly whacked off at an angle. Her pointy elfin ears poked out of her hair. She wore trousers with sharp creases and wide cuffs and silk shirts with long ropes of tiny pearls. Tiny black Mary Janes graced her little feet. She smoked her fake cigarettes with a carved pseudo-ivory holder and blew elaborate smokeless smoke rings around Stevie's head like mists around the Isle of Avalon. Mostly her earrings were discreet diamonds, but when she wanted to dare, she wore big gold hoops and very red lipstick. She egged Stevie on.

But Tate needed Stevie on the planet.

"OK. Well, come back into your body and join this party. We've got 12 hours to go."

Flashback, continued
Nana and William

They'd never spent a night together, but Jolene was in the States, thousands of miles away, Charlotte thought Nana was in the country with Hannah Boone and William had no gigs outside the city of London until June.

To avoid meeting Will's mother on the landing (it was way to soon to bring their families into this) Nana came and went by the backstairs.

Olivia, good downstairs gal that she was, although truth be known she was more financially stable and better educated than both Nana and William put together, did not care about their secret affair, and brought them tea and biscuits and glasses of wine and breakfast in bed as if it were the most normal occurrence in the world and she was happy to keep it from the Old Artist. "Mum's the word," she said, smiling. Beva smiled, too. As she said, herself, "I'm just old, I'm not dead. Or deaf."

But that first night, the night of Nana's arrival, when finally they left their cocoon in Will's bedroom and ventured out on their bikes with picnic to view the moon, that first night found them tongue-tied. There they were, deliciously spent, braced by the fresh air, plastic cups of wine and little crusty sandwiches in their hands. All of a sudden, they couldn't look at each other. There was an embarrassed silence.

Two hours after he'd asked the question, Nana finally said, "I don't know, Will. I don't know if I've come home, I'm not sure where home is, but I am here now."

And so it was.

So, let's leave Nana and William there, for the moment. Let them enjoy their long awaited tryst. Nana also has the "Key to the Key" quest to keep her busy.

And Jolene, too, is busy: with her secrets, her school, her cousins in America, and questions about life, death, the truth and keys.

Let's sort through this other very interesting bit of news developing in Carmel Valley. Nana and Jolene will be showing up at Sweet Farm soon enough, along with their own complicated baggage.

Sweet Farm, Carmel Valley
Deke works up his courage

Deke and Rebecca opened the opposite back doors of the cab at the same time, with similar gestures of impatience: a slight shudder and a squaring of the shoulders. Rebecca got out of the cab immediately, ready to get this next thing onward. She'd had about enough of Michael's backpedaling. He was a stronger and better man than he imagined, and she knew it well. It was time.

While Rebecca was moving toward the Adobe, Deke/Michael sat in the back of the cab with the door open and looked back down the driveway to the rock. *That's where we met, in 1946. Right there!*

I sat there on that turquoise Indian Chief. I heard her shoes scuffling pebbles on the pavement and turned around. Oh man, there she was, just right there. Lord, I remember that moment like it was yesterday. I remember it. From that moment, she was the only one for me. Did she even know that?

That was a long time ago. Maybe she forgot me. Maybe she taught Tate zip about me, so she'd forget me, too.

What in all Glory is gonna happen here? OK, boy. Here we go.

Sadie's House

Esquiline Drive, Carmel Valley Village

The Party

The girls sang country songs and love ballads and silly ditties, potent with meaning. Stevie moved her lips and made the appropriate sounds, but her thoughts were unreadable, rampaging wild beasts. A full-blown fantasy, soundtrack and all (country songs and love ballads and silly ditties, potent with meaning) filled the screen behind her eyes.

The fantasy began with the day she first saw *Adam* in the Outrigger window, to the meeting in the bar, right on into the act itself (which she tried hard to imagine, but bogged down in the coupling and tangling and finally gave up), to falling down, down, down a deep well of love and into a world of dancing in perfect step and offerings of favorite flowers and visions of sweet little houses with white picket fences and gardens and babies and…

Whoa! Stop it! Stop it right now, Stefani Michel! You have gone off the deep end. Settle it right down this minute. Focus on the present.

The present! Oh, good, give Sadie her present. There's a good girl.

Sweet Farm, Carmel Valley
The Visit of Visits Part 3

Rebecca walked through the Adobe House gate and into the garden. She looked up the steps and saw the family gathered in the big open room they called the Middle. She took a breath, turned and looked back toward the gate. She would wait for her son, would not walk up those steps a second time alone.

Rebecca took time to appreciate the fall garden: the tied-back herbs, hardy bushes along neatly kept walkways. Things she did not notice the day before: fruit trees and roses, herbs and flowers for cutting.

Deke straightened his spine as he moved toward her. He squared his shoulders and put on his best public persona. His mother took his arm and they ascended the steps. Jock Wyman was there to open the door. Fox rose from her chair, dazed. Maria, Rita and Fáno stepped back slightly, as if the north wind preceded Deke and his mother into the room and then blew on out the window.

Fox, unable to hold it together another minute, collapsed back into the chair with her quilt. She glanced at Deke, but could not really take him in. She saw a shape and a profile, familiar. He looked at her and looked away. She, too, looked away.

Maria said, "What may I get for you, Rebecca? Tea, perhaps? Coffee? It eez eezy… either way. A sherry, mebbe?" This last with a tiny smile.

"Tea, please," replied her guest, unable to appreciate the innuendo. Maria lifted her chin toward her friend, Juana, in the kitchen, who read the sign for tea. Rebecca gratefully took the chair Jock offered, sat down, removed her hat and gloves and placed them on the table beside her. She looked around the room.

Fox was rolled up like a burrito in her tortilla quilt. She looked pale, like she hadn't slept. No wonder there!

Rita and Fáno stood by the hearth. Maria sat down in her leather and stick chair by the fire, eyes on Deke, then Jock, then Fox. In the kitchen, Juana sliced a little quiche, Felix took some rolls out of the oven.

One look at Deke told Jock volumes. He took Deke's hand in his, suddenly grabbing him up in a hug. "It's good to see you, son. I hafta say, it is good to see you." Suddenly, Jock's thirteen-year build up of anger and resentment disappeared, just lost all its power, like a deflating hot air balloon. He didn't know why. He'd harbored a grudge toward Deke all this time, when he wasn't thinking he was dead. But it wasn't hard at all to see something big had happened to this boy-man.

Deke, in shock, stepped back and looked at Jock's face. He nodded, hugged Jock back, and surveyed the room. One by one, he went to each person. Next, to Maria, who rose to greet him, perplexed by Jock's embrace. She took Deke's offered hand and said, "'Allo, Deke. 'Allo." He had to look away again, from the mother this time.

With Rita and Fáno there was no pretense, no barrier. Their arms were open and Deke went into them as if he had been lost at sea and they were his port in this hellacious storm. He started to cry, which he promised himself he would not do, but somehow the embrace took all the stuffing out of him, all the bravado that got him here this day, and Rita and Fáno would not let him go. Wet minutes went by until Deke released himself from their grasp and wiped his eyes.

Juana brought a hot cup of tea to Mrs. Harley, then she and Felix went to Deke, took his hands in theirs, nodded a silent hello, and quietly left the Wyman clan to themselves.

Breathing was the only sound, and barely audible, as Deke turned to Fox. The long gaze between them bruised the fine red hairs standing straight up on Fox's arms. She felt a pain, like lightning, through her skin, in her blood, in her fingernails and hair follicles, a sorrow too deep for words, for explanations. She saw his face for the first time. She saw him.

As for Deke, through his eyes, Fox was still a girl. She was so beautiful, wrapped up in that old quilt. What did she call it? The Quilt of Colors? *Ah. I remember. She hasn't changed one bit. Still foxy and lean, animalistic, ready to pounce. Still red, softly, all over. Still my Fox.* He squeezed his eyes shut.

After a few seconds, minutes or light years, Deke pulled up a chair and sat down. He did not move toward Fox. He thought she might bolt. He wouldn't blame her. He must look like a danged scalawag.

He actually looked pretty good, considering.

Deke knew he had best get to the point in a hurry. There was no more time to waste.

"I ask you to bear with me here. I'm gonna try to tell this story and keep it all together in a piece, so I am likely to go on and on for a bit. Is that OK?"

He took stock of the situation. Deke's mother sat rather primly in her chair, cup set aside, hands in lap, eyes cast downward with surreptitious glances at her son. Maria had her eye on her youngest daughter, steady and empowering, a gargoyle at the gate of her daughter's fortress. And there was Jock, in his place in the curve of the piano, the host, the ready-to-please, but now, on guard, primed to protect his girls, but his eye on Deke was not hostile.

Rita and Fáno? They gave Deke courage somehow, since the looks on their faces held some forward hope for him, through some sight known only to them.

He turned to face Fox.

"Fox, honey, this is the gist of where I've been. I've been tryin' to boil it down but, I don't know. It won't be boiled. But here it is. At least, what I can say now. "

King City
Deke Interrupted

He *came to* sprawled on his back in a stand of high, dry, razor sharp grasses growing up against a smooth log fence. He'd wet his pants. The second thing he noticed was that he couldn't say his name. He had it on the tip of his tongue, but... dang, he couldn't bring it forth. It hung before him, out beyond the stars in his eyes and the tingle in his skin. The blond hairs on his arms stood on end, and he shivered. He pulled himself up backwards to the fence and sat back against the post. His head hurt like the dickens.

Dang. What? What is this? Worse, I... am...who? Oh, man, I stink. What to do here? Where is this place?

Later, toward dark, after hot hours sweating the sun through his clothes, in and out of consciousness, errant thoughts dropping on the ground, names grasped at here and there just out of reach, he awoke again, mostly from his own aroma: pungent, like smelling salts, not his usual beehive smell, foreign. Toxic. Dried now, but still...

Get, up, man. Me to myself! Hello! Get up... get... up... who?

He couldn't get 'hold of the name. He felt his dry skin with the blond hairs, looked at his clothes: jeans and sweaty plaid shirt, scuffed high-top boots. He looked at his hands, turned his palms up, studied the creases and lines. He turned his left hand over and noticed a white mark on his wrist, where a watch used to be. A mark the shape of a watch.

A watch. My watch. What watch is that? What kind of watch? How do I know what a watch is and not know my name?

He sat for a few more hours, mustering the courage to stand. It was a dark, black sky thick with stars. He tried to stay awake, but his mind wandered and his dreams returned, taking him down through caves of darkness and soft pillows of billowy light. He would float like a specter and then jerk awake, afraid of the dark and the stars, afraid of his moon shadow, his stink, his mind, his deceiving eyes.

It was close to 5 in the morning when he finally bent his knees and twisted around, sore and stiff and bruised of body. He heard his own groan when his head moved through space in slow motion as he turned to face the fence. On his hands and knees now, like a dog, palms flat out on the ground, fingers splayed. He stopped moving. He looked at the rail, the post, the wood.

He felt the dry dirt with his clenched fingers, grabbed a handful of grasses which scraped his palms and knuckles. He stayed like a dog, panting, staring at that fence, but he felt his body sway and knew he had to try standing up or he'd drift off to darkness again and have to start all over.

He lifted his hands off the ground one at a time and held on to the first fence rail. By this time he saw the light breaking over the horizon. *Pretty*, he thought. *Where is that?* He looked steadily at the light, holding tight to the fence, his only support in all the world.

When the body quivered less and the hands steadied and the head became more accustomed to the hurt, pounding away as it was on his brain, he tried another level up. With each level, he braced himself, until his will overcame his pain and, by the fifth rail at the top, he was able to stand. The fence post took all his weight. He leaned against it, gathering his brains and body into a piece. *One piece. I just need to be in one piece.*

He lifted his eyes over the fence. A big dirt lot, or corral or something, barns, empty. He looked to the open space and just wanted to walk there. It was pretty out there. The color was nice. Golden. *Can I walk?* he thought. *One way to find out.*

He didn't push. He swayed a bit with each step. He wanted water. *Why? Why do I want water?* He knew water. It was for drinking, washing. *Washing? That's it.*

Stevie and a Swarm of Bees

The inside of Stevie's head
was buzzing,
full of bees.

From thought
to thought she flitted,
buzzing through
a garden of possibilities,
A forest, a kingdom!

Colors colliding
and feelings expanding
It was exponential.

Before she knew it,
she had a headache,
and the bees
would just not
shut up.

King City
The Letter

He wandered through a dry meadow, aware of cows along the golden hills to the left, taking his measure. He knew cows. He knew he was going south, the sun was still on his left, but higher, but he wasn't sure why.

His feet, baking inside his boots, scuffed through the dirt, stirring up little puffs of dust. He found a narrow path worn by deer or cows or both, he didn't know. But it went somewhere, and he was going there.

It was getting hot; he'd have to find a place to rest soon and get out of the sun. He was thirsty. He kept moving toward a stand of trees.

As he neared the destination, he saw three horses, drinking from a trough. *Holy Mother,* he thought. *Water!*

But he dared not pick up speed, he was barely upright as it was. He trudged forward, feeling the blazing sun on his back, on his throbbing hatless head, his swollen feet. One step. Another step. Finally, he got there: a rest stop for four-legged creatures on the highway to nowhere.

It felt like an hour between the sighting and arrival, but in fact, it took about 20 minutes. The horses, sensing a benign intruder, ambled to the more hospitable shade of the oak trees.

There wasn't a soul in sight. He slowly turned 360° and found it empty of all beings save these three horses and himself. He sat down on the bare dirt and, for the sake of his throbbing cranium, slowly tugged off his boots and socks. He unzipped his jeans and worked his way out. He rifled through his pockets, pulled out a few dollar bills, some coins, a comb and a folded piece of paper and put them on the ground. He slipped his pants into the water trough. He eyed the water and then, he, too, slid in and dunked his head, getting his shirt and underclothes soaked and his skin happily relieved of its acrid scent. He knew he shouldn't drink it, but he let a few sips dribble in while his head was under water. He was so thirsty.

The water hurt his head at first, but he toughed it out, he thought it might help whatever this was, this headache. He'd felt the lump on his head, but didn't have the oomph to wonder about it. It was just a lump. And it hurt.

When he ran out of breath, he burst up through the water, gasping, gagging, spitting. The climb out of the trough was a slippery endeavor, his grasp loose and weak. He retched green water several more times. It took ten minutes to steady his shaking body and put one leg at a time over the side of the trough onto the ground.

He laid his pants out in the sun to dry and found a bit of shade for himself in his shirt and undershorts, knowing the horses would get used to him.

He chewed on a straw and pondered his dilemma. His head pounded, like strong surf against a rock. He counted the little pile of paper money, $18. He knew money. He counted money.

There was something else. He picked up the folded piece of paper—an envelope. A letter, stamped but not sealed, addressed to:

> *Judge Harris*
> *Snippet Sound*
> *Chesapeake Bay MD*

The return address looked like it was just started: *Michael Ha—*

He opened it.

> *July 1950*
>
> *Dear Judge,*
>
> *I am writing about my mother, Rebecca, because she won't. Please, sir, won't you help me get her out of the situation in Oklahoma? I am writing to ask your assistance, as a father.*
>
> *Sincerely, Michael*

1950

Next Stop, King City

He went to sleep again after his lovely horse trough bath. He didn't care. His jeans were freshened, and his skin. He wasn't sure why, but he knew that he had reached one good place, with water. Now, he needed to reach another. As soon as he remembered what it was, he'd go there.

He let himself float along, smelling horse dung and dirt and composting oak leaves. When he awoke, he was face down in dirt with leaves and sticks impressing his cheeks. He brushed his face off and looked up. The horses were gone. *There were horses here before, weren't there?*

The sun moved toward the horizon and his bare legs were cold, so he pulled on his stiff, sunbaked jeans, hot socks and boots. He stood up slowly and walked over to the trough, wondering where the water came from. *Trucked in, I guess.*

Trucked in. From where, exactly? And how do I know this?

He sat on the edge of the trough and contemplated his name. *Smeak. Speak. I don't know. And who's Michael?*

I know my wallet is missing, along with my watch. Wallet. Wallet. Goes in pocket. Money goes inside. I know money. It buys things.

By this time, it had been three days since he had eaten the scrambled eggs he didn't remember, and his stomach grumbled. *Hunger,* he thought. *I know hungry. Money will fix that. I can buy food. How far will $18 go?*

The sun was free-falling toward sundown. He wasn't sure how far he could go, but he thought he ought to keep moving.

There was nothing for him here, except green water. No horses, no food.

He put the wad of bills and the folded letter in his right boot. Something told him it would be safer there.

For the first time, he noticed cars, he knew cars, and decided to head for them. If there are cars, there is a road. A road and cars - people. People, roads and cars, surely there is food.

His feet took him toward food.

Walking at the pace of an addled, pain-riddled octogenarian, he worked out the kinks in his back, gently moved his arms to bring life back into them after so much sleep.

So much sleep? Was I sleeping? And, here? Out in the pucker brush? The only things here are a few cows, and I am sure I saw horses earlier. That trough of water had to be there for horses.

He trudged along, watching the softening sky go from bright blue to robin's egg to pale orange. As he headed toward the road, he saw a big rock by a tree and leaned against it to watch the sun disappear. *If I were west of here, I'd see water. Big water. What's that called?*

At dusk, he made his way to the town. He saw a sign: King City. He saw a poster for the Salinas Rodeo. He remembered something about that. What was it? A girl? Food? He thought of eggs.

He meandered: wavy, irregular, in circles, like his brain, his memory. He saw cafes and a gas station, but couldn't go in. He didn't know what to do, or how to do it. He was lost, stuck in a time warp, a dream. In the dream, his arms and legs worked, but not his brain. He kept looking for his brain. But, he didn't exactly know where to look.

When it grew dark, his fears rose again, and he remembered the last night: cold, wet and full of spooks. His shirt was thin. He had no jacket.

He saw a light, red and glowing. He was by tracks - railroad tracks! Tracks mean trains! Trains mean people, and where there are people, there is food. He followed the tracks and went toward the glowing light.

When he got closer to the light, he heard voices. *This could be good or bad,* he thought. He hesitated, listening. He heard men's voices, laughing, clinking metal, and... *a fire!*

The sound of fire - crackling, hissing - someone threw a log in and sparks flew.

I know fire! Can this be bad? he wondered. *Fire means warmth. Go to it. Now.*

He emerged from behind the pile of metal and walked toward the fire. There were men there, sitting on logs and overturned boxes. One old coot in a grimy duster and floppy hat played a mournful tune on his harmonica. A man seated on a rusty upside-down bucket rose to greet him. The man's straggly beard and missing teeth belied his smiled greeting, "Welcome, Stranger. Warm yourself here by th' fahr. You be a good soul?"

He looked at the man, perplexed. "Good soul?" These words were the first he spoke out loud since waking up back there. *Way back there, when was that? And how long did I sleep? Was I asleep? Good soul. Good soul. I should know the answer to that!*

The fire hissed and crackled in a large can split in half length-wise and lying on its side. The blaze welcomed him, sparkling and warm. He longed to lie down beside it to sleep again. Sleep crept up on him again. *Dang.*

"I, ugh, I… sure. Yes. I think so."

Someone passed him a bottle. Someone else handed him a hard biscuit. He could smell something cooking and his tummy rumbled in response.

There were no more questions. Rules of the Road. Not even his name, which was good, because he hadn't found it. It was right there, though - right on the tip of his tongue, but it tangled up with other things - memories of red hairs, flowers and a sweet smell, like sleep.

A dented tin cup materialized and before he knew it, there was a stringy, thin soup in it and a bent spoon. He groaned with happiness at this simple pleasure of cheap hot soup among men gathered around a fire in a can. He slurped the soup, not caring what the little grey bits and pieces were, it was hot and soothing after a long time without food.

Someone handed him another bottle and they shared it around the circle. He got spiffing drunk but didn't know it and soon slipped off his log onto the ground in a deep sleep. They left him there, covered with an old jacket pulled out of the communal cardboard box, and went to their respective hidey-holes in the yard - behind boxcars, down by the river, in a culvert. When he awoke before dawn, the fire was ashes, ashes, and all the men were gone.

Was that a dream? There were men here, right? The smoldering remnants in the fire pit were real, and the headache, although he was so used to the pain in his head by now the hangover blended right in with the general pounding. And the jacket. He didn't recognize the jacket, but put in on.

He thought the best way to get somewhere was to follow the tracks, they obviously had a destination and that was as good as any until he remembered where he was going and what he ought to be doing, but first he had to find food.

He wandered between First Street and Broadway and Canal Street trying to stay close to the tracks, afraid to go in any establishment and make a mistake. Everything was closed anyway. He reflexively looked at his left wrist for the time. Oh. He had no idea of the time. But he knew time!

He looked at Keebler's Restaurant from across the street for a while, the aroma of the day's baking wafting across his path. He made his way around to the back.

He knocked at the kitchen door. It was opened by a harassed looking middle-aged woman with her hair in a net, bobby-pinned in place. Her red lipstick was half steamed off and damp strands of hair drifted out from under the net. Her loose dress and white apron were dusted with flour.

She looked up and down the street before she spoke to him. "What?" she asked, more petulantly than he thought necessary. He wasn't some bum. He didn't know much at the moment, but he knew he was no bum.

"Work for food, Ma'am? I'm mighty hungry."

He may not have been a bum, but currently he looked and spoke the part like a champ. His blond hair, rinsed in green slime in the horse trough, whipped in the four directions. He had dark circles under his eyes.

"You on somethin'? No drugs here."

"No. No ma'am. I… ah… no."

She looked him over. A decent enough bum might relieve an over-worked woman of her burdensome pots and pans. She took a pack of Camels out of her apron pocket and, scraping a sulpher match across the screen on the door she was holding open with her shoulder, lit it, shook out the match and threw it on the step. *Cigarettes!* He knew cigarettes. He knew that ad - "Camels give me a lift."

She heard him and offered him one of her cigs. He flinched, realizing he'd said that out loud, but took a cigarette and at first couldn't think what to do with it. Then she struck another match and held it in his general direction. He stuck the stick (tobacco!) between his lips and drew breath as she lit the cigarette and threw down the match. Right. He knew this. Smoking.

They smoked in silence for a few seconds: she looked at him out of the corners of her green eyes, he looked at the ground.

She said, "It's danged early. Not even 5. What're you doin' here? Weird time to be job huntin' if you ask me. You drunk?"

"Just hungry, ma'am. I can work for a few hours, I reckon, but my head hurts somethin' fierce, so I may have t'rest. But, could I eat first? I don't remember the last time I ate." Obviously, he forgot the stone soup and two bottles of rot gut of the

69

night before, but he could barely remember anything, and still didn't know his own name, so we won't hold that against him. And sheer hunger made him bold.

"Ha." she said, laughing at his gall. "You don' want much, do ya?"

"Well, no'm. Just food. Just a little."

Swell, thought Madge. *A handsome, stupid, starving bum with no sense of humor.*

"You better come in, then. Cops come round seein' you beggin' this time a day, get you in trouble. I've been here since the crack o'2am, and my helper didn't show up, so you are in big time luck, Mr..... what's your name?" she asked as, after one more glance into the dark night, she let the screen door bang shut behind them.

What'm I gonna say now: I don't know? No. That will not do. He felt the letter scratching his ankle in his right boot.

"Michael Harris, ma'am. My name is Michael Harris."

Madge Darby let the guy in, she didn't know why. She never did that. She knew she shouldn't risk it, working all night alone. No, one didn't mess around with Fate in the dead of night. Who cares if she's 40 years old and looks 60 after a night in the kitchen and feels 100 and over the hill?

But this Michael Harris looked safe to her, maybe not too bright. Slow. Hungry. She sat him by the wood stove where the bread was rising and gave him a thick diner mug of coffee, which he looked at as if it were directly out of the hands of the Creator. She shook her head.

He sat on the stool offered by the woman named Madge and held the coffee with both hands. Coffee! It felt so good to hold it. Calming. He let the steam and aroma waft around his nose.

"You can drink it, ya' know," said Madge, as she ladled the day's soup out of the big pot into a bowl and set it on the counter beside him. The cigarette wiggled and wagged between her lips while she smoked and talked. He watched her cut a slab about an inch thick off the nearest loaf of bread and put it on the counter next to the tomato soup.

"Fresh tomatoes," said Michael. He knew fresh tomatoes! "Thank you, ma'am. Madge. Thank you." Well. He remembered *her* name, at least. She handed him a pot of soft butter.

Why did soft butter make him sad?

He leaned against the sink and washed a thousand pots and pans that morning before he collapsed on a chair by the door and fell into a jerky sleep. She let him. He'd earned the soup and the rest.

The morning staff came in and she said he was her cousin from Memphis and she shook him awake and took him home to her apartment three blocks away and let him sleep on the narrow bed. She was tired, so she took the couch and slept for two hours.

When she woke, he was still sleeping, so she made a tuna sandwich and sat on the couch listening to Spike Jones and the City Slickers on the radio, which he slept through, and he was still sleeping when she left for the cafe at 1:45am.

She was beginning to worry he would sleep his life away, perhaps perish on her new white sheets when, coming home toward noon, she found him sitting up on the edge of the bed looking out the window. He watched two boys play ball.

He looked up and winced when Madge came in.

"Head still hurt?" she asked. And then, "Did you just wake up?"

"Yes, Ma'am and, ugh, yes, Ma'am. It hurts like I had a head-on collision with a herd o' cattle."

She wasn't sure what this meant. She said, "Well, I still need some help, but you have to take the couch, and I think I've got an aspirin, if that'll help."

Deke continues his story

"She was nice, that Madge, so I stayed a few days, I think, I don't know how long, really, or even for sure if her name was Madge, that is just what I remember, but I kept having the feeling I was supposed to follow the tracks, so one day I just up and left.

"By then I had some cash, but still no idea what to do with it, really. Before I walked out the door, I put a loaf of bread under my arm.

"I never told Madge any of my story, 'cause at that time, I was danged confused and was afraid to tell her more than my made-up name. I thought maybe I really was a vagrant, on the run or something, and I thought she might turn me in or think I was crazy or lying or…. Oh, I didn't know what. But the truth is I was afraid of everything right then, so I kept to myself. I'll pay her for that loaf of bread, though, if she's still there.

"I wandered off down the tracks and was picked up in San Ardo, making me a vagrant after all, especially with no wallet. All I had was this letter, and, as I said, it suggested my name was Michael Harris, so I kept the letter in my pocket and adopted the name but still didn't know who I really was or where I was supposed to be.

"Days and weeks went by, I don't know, I ate lots of grey meals in a tin and slept long hours and they let me out because I wasn't causing trouble and hardly said boo to a goose and they sent me on my way, as long as I promised to leave town, and they told me to get some ID. They sent me to the train station with an escort, who showed me how to purchase a ticket. I think they all just thought I was stupid or slow and they were helping me get home.

"So I left, doing nothing about my hurting head because I didn't know there was anything to do. The only address I had that made a connection to anyone was the letter, so I hitch-hiked, walked and took trains and a couple of buses all the way to Maryland, which took forever, because I kept dozing off and missing stops and going to places I don't remember and didn't mean to go. I panhandled for money sometimes. I did more dishes.

"And all that time, there was my name, hanging on a stick in front of me, just out of reach. It made me angry, because it was so close, like it was hiding just around the corner: my name, my life.

"Certain things came back: how to hold a fork, how to spell Mississippi, how to take a bus somewhere, what to do with money. But I was only half there. And the other half had ahold of my name.

"I got there to Judge Harris's house on this place called Snippet Sound on the Chesapeake Bay, near St. Michael's, and, well, they had no idea who I was at first either, but with the letter and all, we figured I was their grandson, Michael Harris Harley, who they never met before, and my mother, Rebecca, their daughter, was somewhere in Oklahoma.

"All this meant nothin' to me at the time. The name didn't ring a bell. I just knew I had a fearsome headache and wanted to lie down in these nice people's home, even on the floor, I didn't care. I was so ready to just lie down."

Deke paused to take a drink of water Jock had placed by his side.

"They took me in right away, this would've been January somethin' in 1951, after I bumped around for months trying to get there.

"Meanwhile, after a week or so, I fell down on the floor and didn't get up. They sent me to the hospital there in Maryland, where I got poked and x-rayed, and they told me I had an abscess on my brain, probably from a hit on the head. I said, oh, yeah, I had a big lump there for the longest time, and it left a hard little knot. But, the most I could remember about it was *comin' to* in a pile of dry brush by a fence somewhere and that I'd wet my pants lyin' there for however long.

"I was in no shape to make any decisions. Heck, I didn't even know my name, so they, the Harrises, went off to Oklahoma to find Ma, out in No Man's Land, in the middle of nowhere, no phone, no nothin'."

He looked across the room to his mother. "Thing is, they found her, and she came to Maryland, and she said later she never would have gotten out of that rattle trap trailer in Oklahoma and gone home if it hadn't been for me, so I guess my letter helped her after all, only it would have been a lot easier if I'd just had a chance to mail it.

"See, my letter was to her father, the Judge. I got it right here. I kept it all this time 'cause till three years ago, it was the only clue I had to … well, anything." Deke reached in his shirt pocket for the letter, folded small.

He looked around the room. "Since Fox and I never got married, and things were so bad in Oklahoma - I know, Fox, I told you we were from Nova Scotia, but it was all so mixed up and grim and sad - I didn't know what to tell you.

"And then you got pregnant. And my mother didn't know about you or even know where I was. I couldn't ever figure out how to tell Ma I couldn't come get her or save her, so I put off telling her about you and my Tate and the family and the farm, and then finally, I wrote the letter to her father, my grandfather, and had it on me the day I got whacked upside the head, or whatever it was, and because of that, they figured out who I was.

"They called me Mike or Michael, so I got used to it, although my mother told me I was always known as Deke in Oklahoma. In Cimarron. I didn't remember that, but it was close enough to Smeak, so I figured we were on the right track.

"I know all this now, but, well, it took a long time to get here. When I got better, I worked on the Woodrow Wilson bridge for a while, but it was too hard for my head, and I had a bad time remembering certain things, which tool to use, so that's when I went to work in the hardware store. I could count screws and sell tools, they just didn't want me plugging them in or anything. Nobody bothered me there, or much cared that I had this mysterious lack of a past, zippity do da, nothing.

Deke drank some water and sat for a moment, his eyes on Fox, who had not moved an inch since his arrival.

"Then one day, about three years ago, I got dizzy and fell off a ladder. I woke up in the recovery room, again, only this time there was good news and bad news."

Deke was full on crying now. Jock handed him a hankie. Deke wiped his eyes and held the handkerchief tight in his fist. Then he looked at Fox's eyes. He choked out the words. His voice quivered with the telling, and by the end, he shook like an aspen.

"Like a flash! Like I'd just woken up from a nap, the first thing I saw in my mind was this cute little face with this crazy mop of blonde curls. *Tatie*, I thought. *Oh my God! Tate!*

"Then, I started crying when I saw your face, Fox. I couldn't quite grasp your name. I saw a foxtail, I thought of foxgloves, I saw your red hair in a blur all around you in a halo. But I didn't get it until I remembered a farm and I suddenly thought that you were still waiting for me in a parking lot in Salinas and I was late. I wondered if it was still hot. I knew you were gonna be blazin' mad because I was late. Then, I could see that I was in a hospital bed and you and Tatie weren't there. My mother was there, and I knew her!"

He tried to stop crying, because it would give him a headache, but he was barely hanging on.

"No one believed me at first, they all kind of thought I'd lost the rest of my marbles in that last fall.

"The bad news was… well, it's all the same. Another surgery, another bunch of stuff pulled from my head."

You could've heard a pin drop.

Deke and Fox stared at each other, locked in space. He slowly pried her trembling hand away from its grip of the quilt's edge. He held her small hand in his two big hands, her precious little hand. He spoke calmly, slowly, difficult when crying and trying to keep from coming unglued in front of your former family.

"So you see, here I am, finally. I had to work out in my mind how to get here, and it all comes back little by little, like trying to remember a complicated dream, and my brain does have some damage, as I say, so I don't think as fast as I used to. I had to get through that last surgery and then I had to let my hair grow back in, which took about a year, but I couldn't see coming here to court you back into my life with half my hair shaved off. And then I started planning how I would get here and what I would do and what I would tell you when I got here, looking at you like this, face to face.

"Yeah, I brought Ma with me, she likes to stick close because, as she says, she never knows when I might fall over. I can put on a good show of strength when I need or want to, but I do tire like an old man."

Deke stopped talking. He kept hold of Fox's hand, softly rubbing her knuckles with his thumb. She still hadn't moved, except to let him take her hand.

The room full of Wymans and their relations was silent while Deke looked down at the hand of his lost love, at the fine red hairs on her arm, the small oval nails at the ends of thin tapered fingers. He looked away again, so afraid was he of what he would find in her eyes.

His head was bent over, his tears quietly dripped onto her hand. He had to look up to dry his eyes, and to dry his eyes, he would have to let go. He didn't move, just kept her hand in both of his.

She saw the tears welling up again in his eyes, for she was looking at him, never wavering now, and as he told his story, it amazed her that, as aligned with him as she thought she was, she did not see. *I knew he wasn't dead. That's all I knew.*

Her own eyes brimmed, and she longed suddenly to mingle her tears with his and make it all go away, all of it, the years, the farm, the family, the pain. Poof.

But thirteen years cannot be denied. And, the shock alone was enough to keep Fox shaking under the quilt. She could only stare at the top of Deke's faded blond head and see his shoulders, shaking, too. She focused on the grey at his temples, the little scar above his right eyebrow. She looked down at his hands.

Fox rose from the chair and grabbed the Quilt of Many Colors around her shoulders. She kept hold of Deke's hand and led him into her parents' room, to the love seat by the fire.

Rebecca nodded and smiled, watching them go. Her smile was thin and kind of tight, but it gave approval, and she was warmed.

"Shall I tell you a story?" Rebecca asked the silent room. "Perhaps I can fill you in on some details."

She told them about life in Cimarron County, softening the blows of grief by minimizing certain grisly details of the drought and dust and death. But she explained to them Deke's wish to see his mother back in Maryland with her kin, something she desired for herself but had been too proud to go home with her tail between her legs much less admit out loud that her life in Cimarron County as a farmer had been a failure. More than a failure. Disaster came to her mind.

As Fox sat with Deke in the other room, Rebecca sipped cold tea and told her version of this story. The red dust would ooze itself out of her pores as they got to know her, she knew, it always did, but she brushed away the grief of Cimarron as best she could and focused on what she had left: Snippet Sound, another ailing son, a bitter woman, and a young girl she'd never met.

Sweet Farm, Carmel Valley
Deke's Letters

The excitement and stress of the day had put Deke to sleep in Fox's arms in about ten minutes. His long legs dangled off the side of the love seat, but he did not seem to mind the inconvenience and softly snored with his head on Fox's shoulder. His blond hair tickled her face.

She focused on that for a moment.

Here she was, arms wrapped around Deke. Here was Deke. Deke Harley, sound asleep, like a baby... like nothing had happened after thirteen years of... what could she say? Total absolute weirdness. Thirteen years!

This was all hard to take in. She smelled his hair, which was longer than before and shaggy. It smelled like sun and baked dust. His neck was warm and sent honey and lemon and leather to her nose and made her think of horses and bees.

She never wanted him to wake up. She wanted to stay right here in this cramped uncomfortable position forever, holding Deke while he slept contentedly, listening to his snore, his inhale, watching his chest rise and fall, waiting for his exhale. She wanted to know each other's thoughts and feelings by osmosis and thought projection, to blend and merge and become one person, never out of each other's reach or sight or smell or hearing again.

A part of her wanted to push him away, tell him to leave her alone, don't come near Tate, haven't you done enough damage for one lifetime? She wanted to shove him off her shoulder and laugh in his face for the absurdity... the audacity of his coming back to Sweet Farm. *Court me, indeed. When Pigs Fly.*

That was a crust around her feelings, like puff pastry on a Wellington.

Fox took her emotional pulse. She pondered the blond head, the scent, the aura of her ... what? Boyfriend? Not husband. Her man.

She focused on the feeling in her gut - a mix of excitement and stomach acid. When had she last eaten? That smelly cheese yesterday? She thought a flock of birds might explode through her navel and fill the sky.

Deke's suede jacket was scrunched open and she noticed a little packet of papers stuffed in his inside pocket. It was tickling his chin, so she gently maneuvered her hand around the front of him to tug it out of the way. When she pulled it free and held it in the one available hand, she could see that it was small envelopes. About 30 of them. *Good Lord. What is this?*

Fox slid her right arm out from behind Deke's back and let him rest against her side. He was conked out, he didn't mind. She had just enough elbowroom to flip through the packet without disturbing him. She squirmed into the bath of light from the window and saw that each envelope had her name on it and a number. *What?*

Should she or should she not open these? They were addressed to her. Could she assume he had them handy to give to her today? Ah, well, she took the plunge and opened #1. What did he call it? Her *foxy little snout.*

Inside was a sheet of perforated and lined paper, pulled out of a notebook and folded about eight times to fit into the little envelope. Some of the edges were folded up.

Her hands were shaking, and his handwriting was small, but she recognized the loops and squiggles.

Dear Foxie,

A few days ago, I came out of a black place I've lived in for a long time. It's like living in a cave that's half lit and it's cold. In that place you did not exist. Neither did Tatie.

There were blanks, like big holes in my mind: spaces before my closed eyes with nothing but shadow figures acting out plays in indistinct whispers. Sometimes I was afraid to fall asleep because there was a cavernous hole in my dreams that often became a big mouth that swallowed me up, a Venus Fly Trap.

I am writing to you now to connect until we meet, if we ever meet. Ma says that I should write, now I've regained some memory. She says it will help me remember more tomorrow if I write down what I've remembered today.

This is what I remember:

You, coming into the bunkhouse that first night - the slim curve of your body under your nightie, which you slipped off pretty quick. It kills me that I did not remember that in these ten years. It ticks me off royally, as a matter of fact. Lots of things have ticked me off in the last few days.

I remember a trip out to the Arroyo Seco Gorge, where we swam next to water snakes and dried off on a big flat boulder and ate tuna sandwiches we'd held out of the water with one hand while we crossed back and forth through the gorge, in the water and over the rocks.

I don't remember how Tate came to be with us, but I do remember her little hands poking at me. I remember your dad, but I don't yet remember his name. Joke. But that's not right.

I think you have sisters.

The doctors say that a memory often needs to be tricked into remembering after amnesia. Sometimes I just pretend to remember stuff. Otherwise people look at me funny.

I had a surgery on my head a few days ago to remove some more debris. I don't know. I'll tell you later, when I remember. My head is half shaved.

Love, Deke Harley

Dear Foxie,

Now that I remember you, I miss you like crazy. For all these years, I missed something, but I didn't know what.

It made me angry, that I couldn't get to it - the loneliness was just there, these little fingers pulling at me, but no faces, no names or bodies.

I can't remember the name of the farm, but I think your name is Wyler, right? See, I'm getting there. I-

No! It's Wyman! You're Fox Wyman! And, if I can remember the name of the farm, I can find you.

Fox, I know it's not my fault, but I'm so sorry I missed the last ten years. It's a crying shame I haven't been there with you, when I know I said I would.

Now I remember we made a promise to "have this baby." I can't remember anymore than this right now, but I know we had the baby, and I know she's Tatie, and I know she's way older now than when I, I guess you'd say, when I left. I'll bet that is what you say.

Oh, Foxie. I hated being in limbo like that, where nothing makes sense. I didn't really know my own mother until five days ago, waking up in bed in the hospital and there she was. Like always. But I jumped up, oh it hurt, I jumped up and hugged her and said, "Ma! Ma! I know you!"

It made her cry, poor Ma. She wanted her son back, and look what she got.

Love, Deke Harley

Foxie,

They pulled the tiny stitches out of my head today.

I remembered something else last night. I remembered you like lavender. Did you have a lavender bush and did we make something from it?

I am home now, at Judge and Mrs. Judge Harris's, my grandparents' house on Snippet Sound.

I have lived here now these 10 years or so, in a little pale green attic room, green like kohlrabi, like celery, with a white bed. The bedspread is chenille, with little nubbly bits forming a pattern, and white-as-white-can-be sheets and these skinny little pillows, like made for dolls. If I want to stand up straight I have to stand in the middle of the room, because, as I said, it's an attic. I share a bathroom with my mother and my Great Uncle Dave who both live on the floor below the attic. Uncle Dave has lived here for more years than anyone can remember - he's my grandfather the judge's brother.

It's a farmhouse built in 1750, with slanted walls and white stucco siding and it overlooks the Bay. I...

Sorry. Head throbbing now. More tomorrow.

Love, Deke Harley

Dear Foxie,

I am thinking about the farm today, I try to remember where and what it is. If I can imagine it, I can imagine you in it, waiting for me and not mad.

I more often imagine you mad, furious. I imagine you looking for me and wondering what the hell happened. I imagine you pushing me out of your mind and forgetting me and getting married and making someone new Tatie's daddy because you think I'm dead or worse, you think I'd leave you.

But, that wouldn't even matter, would it? We were never married, so whatever happened to me, you were free to move on. I should have married you, Fox. I was wrong not to marry you and own up - oh, I know I did. But not full on, you know.

Every day I'm writing these little notes to you and folding them up nice and neat and putting them in little envelopes, as if I were able to walk out to the mailbox and mail them to you.

I'm not sure right now if only half-waking up is good or bad.

Love, Deke Harley

Dear Foxie,

I remembered today when Tate was born. You were so small, they thought they'd have to take her out. You said something like, "No baby of mine will be born like a barbarian," when you thought you were saying, "by caesarian."

You were screamin' and yellin' something fierce, but soon this round chub was born. All that chub in your tiny body.

Right now my memory is like a treasure chest. Every time I open it, I find some new thing.

I cry more now that I'm awake
than I did when I slept through my days
It's because I remember your amber eyes
And think of your funny ways

You're light of body and red of hair
All over your skin it glows
I remember kissing you
all the way down
From your red head to your toes

Love, Deke Harley

Carmel Valley

Tate and Stevie Ride Home With Farley

While Tate prattled on about the slumber party singers and songs, oblivious to her cousin's inner turmoil, Stevie's fantasy life blossomed into a full-fledged love affair.

She imagined a story for *Adam*: his hair suggested Swedish or Nordic blood, the clothes (jeans, leather jacket, white shirt, brown polished boots tooled with a dragon pattern) were nice, so he was educated, or rich, or both. He spoke well, slightly country.

I didn't even ask him how he made a living! But, no, that's not important here. The less I know the better. But what if it's love? Shut up!

Tate and Stevie

The Wymans planned to whisk Deke and Rebecca off the Sweet Farm premises before Tate and Stevie arrived home that Saturday, but it didn't work out that way. These were no crumbs to brush off the table. They sent the cab driver home with a big tip and no story for Mabel.

Fox and Deke were still by the bedroom hearth, where Deke continued the deep sleep of the unburdened soul. Rebecca napped in Jolene's room (her nap tended toward the fanciful, as she lay there on Jolene's bed, aware of the half sun and blue sky/half moon and stars painted on the ceiling). Maria napped in Nana's room (ah, her sleep was all Frenchified, as Stevie might say: satisfied and strong, looking forward to an afternoon espresso and further no-nonsense resolutions to this latest family cliffhanger). Jock moved to his den with a snifter of warm brandy, put his feet up on his desk and pondered, dissected and cogitated over Deke Harley's fantastic tale.

Rita and Fáno, patting each other on their respective butts, went into the kitchen to clean up and decide what to do about Tate and Stevie's impending arrival. Someone would have to meet them at the gate.

An hour later, after a fortuitous warning from Sadie's mother, Tate and Stevie were on the way with the long-suffering Farley Simpson, who was dying to talk to Stevie about her encounter the day before with her Perfect Stranger, but he knew his chances of that were zipped until their usual bed-time phone call, eons from now.

Stevie avoided looking Farley in the eye, which irritated and concerned him. And she put Tate in the middle of the truck's bench seat, which he also found impossible and ridiculous, because he couldn't talk to Stevie at all on the way home. And then, she focused her own attention on the fascinating landscape whizzing by the passenger side of the truck, which ticked him off no end. Usually she cut through Tate's chatter with some funny question or nugget of obscure information, like how the castrati of the 18th century actually kept their high boyish voices, which directed them off on some other amusing avenue of teenaged conversation.

But she was suddenly shy to talk to Farley about her Perfect Stranger. Why? Perhaps because she had given him a name, made him real, conjured up for him a life and genealogy. Oh, yes! A proper family tree, complete with a measurable drop of royal Habsburg blood, a coat of arms having something to do with dragons and a horse thief on his father's side.

But she'd deal with Farley later. And, as yet she was unwilling to reveal to Tate, her cousin and best girl-pal, this personal fire-walk, this pro-active and admittedly provocative act she was contemplating.

Tate, who had been mostly awake all night… was just ready for a nap.

Farley pulled his truck, a 1950 Chevy pickup, rakishly painted a luminous burnt orange and spit-shined every morning by the ever-spit-shining Farley, into the Sweet Farm driveway. He saw Rita and Fáno waiting for them by the Adobe House gate.

That seemed odd to Farley. Those two were always doing something constructive, not standing around gates looking serious. And it was just plain not like them to be frowning and whispering. They usually looked like cats that had just lapped cream, all happy and smiling, purring. They weren't frowning here, exactly, but not their usual selves.

Stevie opened the truck door and slid off the seat and out of the cab, followed by Tate and a pile of duffels and bedrolls. The girls were in a laughing kerfuffle while untangling the bags, but when they looked up at Rita and Fáno, they detected monumental news. The universe lost its voice. Monastery quiet. Laryngitis quiet. A strange smell hit their nostrils, green and out of season, like lawn mower cuttings of spring grass. They thought there might be bad news when they tried without success to read Stevie's parents' faces.

Farley thought to leave but was waved to stay by Fáno, who gently herded the young girls with an arm around each over to the little table. Farley and Rita followed and in a moment, all were seated.

"Leetle onez," Fáno began, "although you are not so leetle now, I know, and so we will treat you like ze young adults you are and tell you what haz occurred at Sweet Farm. A miracle haz happened thees day."

Both girls looked relieved. Tate could hardly keep her eyes open and Stevie barely kept up with the conversation for her own fantastical reasons, but they were glad it was good news.

Great, Stevie thought. *Tell us something good and then we can go fall down on our beds.*

Rita and Fáno both looked at Tate, who squirmed in the spotlight. "Did something happen? Is my mom OK? Why are you looking at me, Aunt Rita?"

Rita said, "Honey, Fox is just fine, but something amazing happened today that will pretty much knock your socks right off into next week, so I am just going to say, hold onto your hat."

"You're mixing idioms, Mom. I'm confused."

"Stefani Awena Michel, stay with me here. This is a life changing event, not a literary opportunity or a comedy routine." She looked into Stevie with her X-ray vision. This got our girl's attention — it caused a little shiver down the spine and raised the hairs on her arms and a chill in her veins. Plus, the use of Stevie's full name meant Rita was all business.

Rita and Fáno shared the headlines, gently bringing the story to the girl most affected by the news. Tate listened intently for a few minutes, looking from Rita to Fáno and Fáno to Rita, like their words were tiny tennis balls, bouncing back and forth (ping, ping, ping, ping). She lost track of the details they were sharing, because all she heard was Deke is alive. Ping, ping. Your father, Deke is here. Deke is alive. Alive. Ping, Ping. *My father is alive and here. My father is alive.* Ping, Ping. Alive. Alive. Ping, ping, ping.

Stevie looked at her friend and cousin. She wondered if Tate would faint. I might, in the situation, thought Stevie. This is worthy of a dead-away faint.

But Tate held herself together with as much dignity as she could muster, considering, and did not burst into monster tears.

You see, Tate had been preparing for this moment all her life, give or take. What does a young girl do regarding a missing father besides believe in his return? As Stevie so eloquently once said, and Tate paraphrased in her mind often as a kind of mantra, "Dead is dead, but missing means he might come back."

And here he is.

Tate sat silent and immobile at the little outside table by the Tea Room with her aunt, uncle, cousin and Farley. She looked at the fading fall plants along the barn wall: cineraria gone to seed, Hostas curling brown edges, red valerian blowing dandelion-style puffs of tiny seeds around the neighborhood, invading. She imagined the fingers of roots moving through the ground. She let her mind go, making pictures of obscure things: seeds, plants, barn door, truck, resting in this amazing news that her father was home, right over there in the Adobe House. *We are separated by a wall of adobe.*

Farley left for Salinas with advice to keep this under his Stetson for the time being, until they figured out what to tell the outside world.

Farley now had two major Sweet Farm dramas on his mind: his best girl friend Stevie's imminent introduction into the joys of nooky with a Perfect Stranger and now, the return of Deke Harley, which must have Tate and Fox and everyone in the biggest shoe drop of all time - the one they've all been waiting for. Well, three Sweet Farm dramas, if you include Jolene's Mysterious Key, but fortunately, he had no direct involvement with the Key thing. Just the gossip by way of *you know who.*

Farley wasn't sure how much more he could hold in his brain, considering he had homework and his dad and his college hunt and all, but he was certain to get an earful from his best friend on the phone tonight. *She won't be able to stand it! She'll call me.*

But first, let's follow Tate and Stevie as they make their way to the Hobbit House, where they climb up and sit in the big

Yellow circle, their Switzerland, neutral territory, their Middle, to contemplate this latest change in status. Tate has a father in the flesh.

Stevie's own little secret still filled her consciousness: *Adam's* face, *Adam's* voice, *Adam's* hands, and she now had the added worry that all this Deke Harley business might prevent her excursion to Cannery Row tomorrow and ruin her perfect timing and then she chastised her selfish self for her self-centered ways.

She had no way to contact her Perfect Stranger, except maybe at the bar at the Outrigger, but it was unlikely he would be there waiting for her call. And who would she ask for? Is there anyone there fake-named *Adam*? How was he going to let her know, anyway? Did he have super powers? *Ha. He's probably gone home to his wife and child. I didn't even ask him if he was married.*

She was uneasy now and got out her colored pencils and journal to stay occupied until Tate was ready to talk.

And even if she wants to talk, I'll have nothing to say. Because all I can think about is Adam. *And all she can think about is Deke. I am a terrible friend.*

Tate *was* thinking about Deke. But she was also thinking about her mother, and how Fox took the news: what she did; what went through her mind; if she thought about her, Tate; did she flip out or hold it all in?

She tried to imagine what he would look like, but she had no reference so she conjured up the equally tragic figure of James Dean, her default stand-in for the real thing. More tragic, as it turns out, since he died. Tate couldn't get the James Dean image past about 25 years old, so that didn't apply. Especially if Deke was wounded. *Getting wounded must age a person*, Tate thought.

Over the years, Tate concocted elaborate stories about her father. No one told her anything, so she was creative: Deke was a secret agent; Deke, the cowboy burglar on the run; Deke, dropped in from Pluto, making her half Plutonian, which explained her misfit-ness. She never wrote down her thoughts, but she knew that he was alive and that whatever his story was, it was going to be very different from her imagined reasons for abandoning their family. In fact, it had better be the best story ever told, or she would personally smack him.

Why? Because it had destroyed her mother's life, that's why. Fox Wyman was a shell of a person, and it irked Tate like crazy sometimes that this one person had such a grip on her mother. *It's all so confusing!*

Fox knew he was alive, too. A couple of years before, in a brief moment of intimacy (few and far between with this mother and daughter), Fox admitted to Tate that she absolutely believed Deke was alive, and that was the most painful part, because it meant he could leave her. Leave them.

But this story? Well, this topped them all. If we can believe him.

"Do you believe it, Stevie?"

"What?"

"Deke Harley. Do you believe his story?"

"Oh. Why wouldn't I believe it?"

"I don't know. It just seems pretty far-fetched. Ten years is a long time to have amnesia."

"Now, how would you know that? Have you ever studied amnesia? Had amnesia?"

"No.o.o.o...."

"Well, then, what do you know? Besides, his mother is involved. Would she make this up? She sounds like a lady."

"Yeah. Well. Maybe. I'm just saying that he could be lying. Drifters lie all the time, don't they?"

"I think you mean grifters, hon. Drifters just move around a lot. Grifters are out to cheat you."

"Uh huh."

"Well, anyway, Fáno would tell you to hold your judgment until you see him. When's that going to be?"

"I don't know. Later tonight, I guess. When they come up for air."

"Ooooh. Gnarly. Are you mad? Aren't you excited? Happy?"

"I don't know what I feel, Stevie. He shows up out of the blue and changes everything."

Home

Felix, Juana and Chico, now a six-year-old gentleman, brought the Harley's bags home from the Monterey Downtown Hotel as dusk laid its soft little blanket over the Sweet Farm inhabitants. It was clear that Rebecca Harris Harley and her son, Deke, Michael, whatever you want to call him, had some business with the family, were family, so naturally, they would stay at Sweet Farm.

Rebecca, grateful for the open-hearted welcome of the complex Harleys by the Wyman family, emerged from her nap in Jolene's room and spent a few moments with Maria before any of the others re-entered the stage of this, what had Rita called it? *Life Changing Event.*

"I cannot tell you, Maria, how grateful I am you have reacted so warmly to Michael, er, Deke's story. You can see he is changed."

"Indeed he is, Rebecca. He is a different man, but still himself. Oddly, I think he's kept all the sweet parts and lost the brashness. I miss his smile, though. I wonder how all theez can possibly be? It's an incredible story. And for so long! More than ten years to even begin to know his life again. And you. How did it go for you? How must it be to see your son go through theez? You must have had so many, many painful moments."

Rebecca and Maria held each other's gazes — they touched spirit to spirit, as women do, lifting their cosmic burdens and exposing the soft vulnerable parts, the underbelly of motherhood.

They sighed in harmony. Whoever caused the bump on Deke Harley's head could be anywhere by now - incarcerated for some minor infraction, fathers of wayward children or graduated from college and medical school and maintaining lucrative offices in Monterey. Maria and Rebecca read each other's minds and hugged for the sake of their children.

Jock walked into the room just then, followed by Rita, Juana and Chico, a little human caravan carrying Rebecca's bags up the front steps and into the Adobe and on into Nana's room.

Tate, who a few hours earlier had arrived home from the slumber party ready for soft sheets, her fluffy pillow and a particular stuffed animal, was wide awake now and expecting to meet her long lost father.

Fox and Deke Don't Talk

Contrary to the mixed-up Tate's view, Fox and Deke were not having a sensual time of it, greeting each other in close embrace. They were in the Barn apartment alright, side by side in their bed of old, propped up on pillows, on quilts Deke remembered with a slight moan somewhere between pain and joy.

Deke had awakened in Fox's arms in Jock and Maria's room. By then, Fox had read all the letters, which fell to the floor and scattered as she, too, dosed off. Deke grunted and Fox's eyes blinked open. They looked at each other full-on for the first time and couldn't look away.

Fox simply said, "Come on."

They gathered up the letters and made their way out the little back door without running into anyone. If the thirteen-year build-up to this hadn't been so excrutiating and heart breaking, they would have laughed. But, it was no time for laughs. Not yet. There were hearts to mend, grieving to un-grieve.

They sat silent as monks, perplexed as push-me-pull-yous. They couldn't hold hands, or touch: too intimate, familiar, foreign, scary.

Jock, at his desk in the little den, looked out the window while swirling brandy in the snifter (Jock did much more swirling than drinking). He saw the reunited no-longer-young lovers tiptoeing out to the Barn and hoped the best for this reunion.

Tate and Stevie

Tate finally conked out in the Hobbit on her pile of pillows after a lengthy conversation about found fathers, so Stevie sat back on her cushion and stole a few moments to contemplate her Perfect Stranger.

She toyed with the strands of plastic beads draped along the low ceiling. She nestled into her personal space in the Hobbit, looking intently at the elvish writing on the wall. Today it said, *You will have happiness in love.* Uh oh.

The girl cousins were sprouting into women, and their refuge must change too, change or be abandoned, like old toys. The Hobbit House had no more dignity than ever: wild with tinsel and baubles, drawings, fetishes and corn husk dolls, but it held their growing spirits.

Tate filled her cubby with throw pillows of many sizes, soft squishy things in which to burrow, like a rabbit. And her basket, for the future singer and her band: guitar strings, bandana, sequined tube top, hope.

Stevie's giant cushion, made from the stuffing of several old pillows and a flannel sheet, filled her Hobbit House cubby like a fat futon. When she pulled her tiny writing table over, the pillow bed squished up nicely behind her fanny. She fit perfectly.

Jolene's decor tended to float, like Jolene. On her visits, she pulled in pillows from beds and sofas from around the compound and made her nest anew. She didn't mind. Her visits grounded her, gave her family. Not to diss Grand Mama Charlotte. Or her mother, Nana. But, the Hobbit House, the cousins, Sweet Farm, just made sense to Jolene. Even though her father died nearby. And she chose to go back to England to finish school at Woolsley. It was hard to explain.

All three girls have hard things to explain.

Stevie thought, *I could still go to Cannery Row in the afternoon tomorrow, maybe go to the Barn with Tate later tonight to meet Deke. To meet Deke! Wow! Rita's right. This is amazing!*

What shall she wear tomorrow? Something easy to remove? No, too obvious. Besides, she has to look like she's going to apply for a busgirl's job at Warehouse Pizza, not out for sexual congress with a mystery man some years her senior.

He's not that much older, she thought. *Just weathered by life. All that Habsburgian blood must make life full and interesting, traveling all over the world being famous for twelve drops of the ancient blood of the glitterati.*

She was laughing at herself now, once again pulling in the reigns of her wild horses racing off to love. How many times had she wagged her finger at herself over this in the last 24 hours? Dozens! *Calm down!*

Her conflicts were having a chase around the table - love and sex got in the way of each other, which she knew would happen. *Now what have I done?*

Rita Takes a Nap

After Rita and Fáno told the girl cousins about Deke's return, there was really nothing for Rita to do, nothing she could do, except go home and sit for a while. She escorted the girls over to the Hobbit, where they had resolved to consider the implications of this newsflash, and then walked the path to her own front door, where she took off her boots, slipped into knitted socks and went to the kitchen for a cup of strong black tea.

Rita sat her little self down on the sofa, alone now for the first time in 24 hours, when this chapter in their family saga first unfolded. She pulled the crocheted forest green afghan over her knees and curled up in the corner of the L shaped brown velvet sofa, pulling a fat pillow from the pile to hold like a teddy, close to her chest, for warmth and cheer.

She sipped her tea, set the cup down on the triangular coffee table and snuggled in deep. Like everyone on the compound, she snatched a few moments sleep, letting the burdens she had carried this day drift away. She slept, and dreamed she was a little girl on the Ark, responsible for naming all the animals as they entered the boat up a wide ramp, two by two. Not turkey, or hog, or giraffe, but Herb and Kathy, Peter and Martha. The animals began to jump into the boat before she could hang around their necks the ribbons with medals stamped with John, or Selma or Joan. She was a worried little girl, trying to stay up with her job and failing miserably. She looked around to find the person who would reprimand her, and discovered she was alone on the boat - the sole human with four thousand pairs of animals: Richard, Penelope, Thomas, Jane.

When she awoke, it was with a sudden urge to bring Tate and her long lost father together. She splashed water on her face and walked to the Barn.

The top half of the Dutch door was open, so Rita tapped and went in. She moved through the tiny living room to the door of the tiny bedroom and peeked around the corner in her little unobtrusive way.

Look at them. Rita was amused by the whole thing by now: two scared rabbits sitting there.

This is a glorious thing! she thought. *Be happy!*

They should at least be holding hands, but there they lay, still as stone, arms at their sides, avoiding the touch of the other.

The intimacy of the earlier nap made them awkward now. Fox couldn't believe she'd spent the morning holding Deke Harley while he slept.

"You two OK in here?"

"Yes. Sure. Come in, Rita." Fox's voice quavered. *Not fine. Faking fine*, Rita thought.

Rita stepped into the room and sat on the end of the bed.

"Your daughter is waiting to meet you, Deke."

Saturday Night on the Compound

Rita said, "Time enough to sort out all these complex puzzle pieces tomorrow, and the next day and the next. There's a young girl in the Hobbit House who has been waiting for this all her life."

When summoned, the girls walked over to the Barn together, holding hands. The closer they got to the Barn, the stronger Stevie's impulse to let Tate go in alone, to meet her father and be with her family unit of three without a witness. It was so private. There was no place for Stevie in this picture. Not yet. She hugged her friend and cousin and looked into her eyes and turned away.

Tate went in and closed the door behind her. Stevie considered staying near for support, the top half of the Dutch door was open, she could hear if Tate got upset or anything. But no… leave them to it.

She walked over to the Adobe where, to her great starving teenaged happiness, a platter of cold turkey and salad was on the big table. She piled a little on a plate and went to the Hobbit to nibble some food, drink cold tea and finally have a few uninterrupted minutes alone in which to dream her dreams and fantasize over her initiation into the wonders of love-making.

Oh, she wasn't forgetting her loyalty to her cousin and what Tate was going through right now, but there was nothing she could do to help at the moment, so she could take a break to indulge her imagination.

Stevie's feelings had changed from intellectual curiosity to being profoundly moved, from complete control to managing an uncomfortable and uncharacteristic swoon. All this took place in the last 24 hours, and all inside her head. Well, it included many parts of her body. After a half an hour in the company of the Perfect Stranger, Stevie understood Aunt Nana's phrase, "Love is blind and sex makes you stupid." And she hadn't even had the sex part yet!

Rather than enjoying the anticipation of the morrow, Stevie began to worry that her plan had backfired already, and she could no longer trust herself. She was too analytical to allow this to happen. She'd have to call it off.

But, this is the most extraordinary feeling, this buzz, this vibration of all the senses. It's worth it for this, this expectation. Maybe I won't call it off. How could I anyway? I'd have to show up there long enough to say I had changed my mind, so I may as well show up and… see what happens.

Stevie got into her bed and dialed Farley's number, just like he knew she would. *This is what allies are for*, she thought. *You have to be able to say anything to them. I have bottled this up long enough, and explosions are such messy ways to release tension. I'll have to tell him. I'll have to tell him everything.*

Oh, Lord. No, I can't. I can't! How can I tell him how this feels? She disconnected the call and kept her finger on the button as though that would sever the near indecent exposure. For it would be indecent. Just the lightning thrill of the imagined touch of the Perfect Stranger was enough to prove that. She was over the top.

OK, she could call Farley, but could she talk without revealing her quivering hips? Lips? It doesn't matter. She's such an easy read with Farley, unfortunately. Could she toss it off and plead friendship, tell Farley that between the very busy birthday party and now Tate's newest plot twist, why, she hadn't even had time to think about it?

"I still say you've lost your noodle," said Farley after she'd told him as much as she dared. She could tell he didn't believe her cool attitude, her nonchalance. She was sorry now she ever told Farley any of it. *Why do I have to tell him everything?*

She wished she could take it all back, rewind the tape. But, as it was out there in their shared universe, she could only pretend that it was a small thing and not expose the monumental force of life she felt in her belly.

Words are like fingers pointing at the moon,
not to be confused with the moon itself.
- Japanese Proverb

November 1963
In the Barn Apartment
Sweet Farm, Carmel Valley

Tate's tongue was tied in one hundred knots and she was busy imagining her own begetting. Need we even say it was the most blissful and confused and striking moment of Tate's sixteen years to date?

Outside the bedroom window, nature's orchestra chirped a welcome home chorus as the sparrows and starlings settled into their cypress tree for the late afternoon song to sunset. Some lined up along the wires, like the Carmel Bach Festival Chorale.

Deke remembered those sounds. And Fox's rhythmic breathing in the night, and her sudden intake of breath at a certain responsive moment when they met together, man and woman.

Deke remembered Tatie's 2½ year-old baby voice, "De-De, me!" Grabbing his finger and pulling him out of bed. He remembered her baby laugh.

Deke's mind overflowed with tiny details of the years with Fox and Tate and the rest of the family on Sweet Farm, like a pump filling him up after years of drought and famine in the desert of his thoughts. He lay on the bed and looked at their feet: his and Fox's socks, Tate's bare toes, their jeans. When he left in 1950 (he'd better find a new phrase, it makes it sound like he did it on purpose and there was nothing on purpose about it, except that part about one step at a time)... when he disappeared (not much better, but it would do for now), Tate wasn't even two feet tall. Now, the image of her mother, only blonde. And taller. But the lean angular body just lacked the fine red hairs all over to be exactly like Fox.

"Do you remember me at all, Tatie?"

Fox had left the room to find food, there being a collective need for protein.

Tate turned to look at her father, taking him in for the first time. When she arrived at her mother's bedroom door, she was so embarrassed, she could hardly look at him.

Why, he wasn't at all like James Dean. Why did she ever think that? James Dean was all carved and moody, sexy slick hair and squinting half-smile.

This man, this real-live Deke Harley, this thirteen-year-missing-father, was not only a complete stranger who fit no story she ever imagined, but was kind of sweet and soft... blurred, like through a filmy chiffon. His wavy blond hair shagged around his head and ears and gave his face a vulnerable, innocent look.

"I remember certain things. But, no one talked about you, so it faded. I was pretty young. Not even 3. I remember stars. And I remember DeDe. That was you, wasn't it?"

"Yes." Deke looked about to cry. *Dang*, he thought. *Stop the tears, already.* "You used to get up in the middle of the night."

"I'm still up in the middle of the night. But, Fox isn't you, like you."

He smiled at this.

Oh, Lord, he smiled! It lit his eyes. It brightened the room. The sun came out.

"She doesn't go outside and lie under the stars with you?" Tate shook her head, distracted by the sheer power of his teeth. Did he know? And then, the smile was gone, replaced by time and sorrow.

"That's all I thought about, lying in a hospital bed that last time, after you came back to my mind. All I could see was this pretty little girl, banging on pots and pointing at the sky. When I thought of Foxie… when I thought of your mom, all I could see was red. I could see the red fuzz by her ears. And I could see that funny bend in her rusty hair. I saw her bare feet and red-painted toenails. But you, I could see you perfectly.

"Look at you now. No little girl." Tears were spilling fast now. "I missed so much, Tate. I'm so sorry."

"It's not your fault. And you're here now." *Where's that smile? I want his smile back! I've waited all these years for that!*

"All those years, Tatie, all that time, I had this longing for something. It was always just out of reach, just lurking at the back of my mind. I felt it, close sometimes, its sweet breath on my cheek, like it was a thing. Like if I turned around really fast, I would see it, I would see what I missed."

Tate looked at this man they said was her father and fathomed the unfathomable. "Can I play you a song?"

Stevie's Saturday Night continues

Stevie hung up the phone in a huff after an unsatisfying conversation with Farley, usually the voice of reason and Stevie's great champion: Lancelot carrying her ribbons into battle. But he was being difficult. And argumentative. *Unreasonable. Ugh! Nosy!*

She was restless and hungry. She shuffled in her slippers to the Chapel House fridge and took out peanut butter and blackberry jam and put them on the counter. In the "Baker's Drawer" of the pantry, she lifted out a loaf of bread, took it out of the bag, cut two pieces and slathered them with PB&J.

She thought about Farley's accusations and agreed with most of them - yes, she was being selfish, but there was a timing issue, never mind; yes, she was taking risks; yes, this was a big time for Tate. Blah blah! She knew all that.

But, how could she explain to Farley that this is a once in a lifetime opportunity? How could she describe to a mere boy (who was two years older than she, a senior, and choosing a college) what the feeling was that slid through her veins, that tingled her hair, that twinkled in her eyes? She tried to keep a lid on the more fanciful imaginings, but she had the most beautiful ideas of love filling up her senses. She could see it in her fingernails; they were pink with love. She felt it in her eyelashes, wet with the tears of love. She knew where it started and she thought she knew where it ended. Her innards were spinning like tops. Is this love?

She was just sitting down at the counter with a glass of milk, taking bites out of her PB&J, when there was a light tap on the front door. She heard the outer door open and the scuffle of someone drying shoes on the mat.

Stevie looked up as the inner door opened, not sure whom to expect: Rita or Fáno wouldn't knock, since they lived here, Tate would come to Stevie's bedroom door and just slide in, and it was a bit late for visitors.

What she saw gave her the fright of her life. Her intestines tied themselves into a knotty pretzel and churned its contents.

"Wh… What. Are. You. Doing. Here?" *Oh my God, this can't be real!* Stevie thought, suddenly scared. *This is downright creepy! How did he find me?*

Her stomach rumbled and cried out for help.

Then Tate stepped from behind the man, from behind *Adam*, and smiled.

"Stevie, meet my dad, Deke Harley."

Stevie flew to the bathroom and threw up. She hovered over the toilet, retching over and over, until nothing else could possibly be released. All her dreams of love. All her fantasies. All her desire spun down the flushing toilet with her PB&J sick.

Tate was by her side in a moment with her father close behind. "Make him go away," Stevie whispered. "I'm sick. Maybe the peanut butter. Please. I'll… I'll meet your father later. Please. Make him go away." And then she turned back to the toilet and lost more and more of nothing. Of everything.

It took *Adam*/Deke/Michael Harris Harley, a minute to realize who was throwing up. When Tate lifted up the long dark braid to keep it out of the way of the exploding sickness, he knew.

It was the girl from the Outrigger. *Sam*, not Stevie.

Oh Lord. This is Stevie.

He turned and left the Chapel House before all dignity was lost forever.

Stevie, as Low as it Gets

In this not so subtle twist of fate, it was Stevie's turn to hide out in her room. It made her think of Nana and Chuck, how they had navigated their relationship in a conjoined muteness; of Jolene, holing up in her room upon arrival three years ago. They understood silence.

What would have, could have been the most glorious day of her budding adulthood was now dashed and broken, a mess, a huge, potentially very embarrassing colossal botch.

Stevie's mind was extremely crowded. Her muses and critics gathered there, jockeying for position. The critics, the loudest, shook their pointy fingers at her folly. The critics usually appeared in nun garb: they had the pointiest fingers. Her parents wouldn't criticize, but the disappointed looks Stevie imagined were especially withering. Tate would roll her eyes, if it weren't her father in question. As it was her father in the center of this mind-boggling turn of events, Stevie was hoping Tate would be the last to know.

The muses didn't need to be loud. They lounged on Stevie's shoulders and crossed their legs, using the smoke of their fake cigarettes to write messages in the sky for Stevie. They laughed at her folly, for when the muses joined forces, it was general hilarity at Stevie's expense. Imagine two muses. In cahoots.

The other one, the blonde one, known as Fly, carried a lighter satchel than Patricia's, paraphernalia of the higher realms. She did, yes, have wings, big butterfly affairs, full of buttery colors and wavy patterns: her attire was floaty and loose for butter-flight, better lift for the hovering pale rainbow arc she scored high above Stevie's beleaguered head. When Patricia invited Fly to the muse lounge, watch out! Salt and Pepper!

Which is better? Pointy fingers or laughter? Both are hard to take when they are focused on you. Stevie did not find this funny in the least. She was more than upset. She was devastated. She was destroyed. At 15, her life was over. She would never leave her room again, never show her face in public. Ha! Public? Who cares about the public? No. This shame was centered right here, at Sweet Farm. Just her entire family.

Did he tell? No.o.o.o.o! Would he? No.o.o.o.o! Was he laughing? Does Tate know? Has Farley called? Oh God! She wished she had never opened her big giant Joe E. Brown mouth.

She told her parents it might be food poisoning: throw that peanut butter away! Innocently, they buffered her from the world, although they did think the peanut butter was ok.

Stevie's heart was broken. Her pride dashed to bits. Her folly bright in neon lights for all the Sweet Farm world to see. Her legs no longer wobbled with desire but with cringing embarrassment. How could she ever face Deke Harley? No, she would have to avoid him for the rest of her life.

And Farley! What on earth would she tell him? She might have to avoid him, too. Forever. *Maybe he'll forget we're friends, he has a lot on his mind.*

Stevie curled up on the little sofa in her room, having tossed and turned in her bed sheets to their considerable disruption, destroyed by the cyclone of the broken-hearted. She looked out the window and watched bugs crawl over tiny branches on the graceful bushes brushing up against the window. The bug universe. So tiny. So free. So not embarrassed.

Stevie fought back nausea every time she thought of Deke Harley's face, *Adam's* face! His beautiful face, the moment he realized who she was.

Throwing up! She was throwing up when the Man of her Dreams, the Awakener of Joy, discovered her true identity.

I simply cannot believe this is happening to me.

The Awakener of Joy is my uncle!

Deke Interrupted - Part 2

*Home is the place where, when you have
to go there, they have to take you in.*
– Robert Frost

November 1963
Sweet Farm, Carmel Valley
Fox's Saturday Night

Fox examined the wood grain in the wall. She'd never noticed those patterns before. She considered her mother's story of the ancestor whose last days were spent in a wingback chair in the family dining room, counting bricks in the wall. When asked why, she said, "It keeps the bad away."

If there were bricks, Fox just might be counting them.

She lay next to the man she loved, once loved, and watched the movie of her former life on a screen behind her eyes and between her ears. Hank Williams crooned her long time mantra, "I'm So Lonesome I Could Cry." She hummed it at night, hoping to lull herself to sleep with sweet remembrance, but all she ever got was more lonesome.

Fox wallowed in visions of long-ago times (not forgotten - pushed away, but not far enough away to be forgotten), memories of her sweet secret months with Deke, when she tiptoed barefooted out the back door and around to the bunkhouse. She clearly saw, in her busy mind's eye, the sheer joy when the three of them lived in the Barn apartment, the family they were.

By the time Rita came into the room with Tate, Fox was exhausted from holding the stressful stillness. None of this made sense. She sat with Deke asleep with his head on her shoulder for two hours. But, as the shock wore off, the body and mind adjusted to the reality, and Fox began to doubt.

Fox and Rita sat now on the edge of the very bed, holding hands. Fox was trembling. Her eyelashes hurt. Her face felt like a mask she needed to peel off. Her jeans were tight, shrunk by madness.

Deke and Tate were together somewhere on the compound.

"I'm certainly not ready to have him in this bed, I don't care if it is the same bed we slept in forever ago. In fact, because it is the same bed. We bought this bed together!

"This is all too fast, too soon, Rita. I don't even know who he *is*. I only know who he *was*. 24 hours ago he was still AWOL! He was *'presumed dead!'* We were together less than four years, Rita. Thirteen years later, we do not, cannot just pick up where we left off."

She let go of Rita's hand and fidgeted with the hem of her sweater. Her long nails worked the threads loose and she started to pull. Rita took her sister's hand back, to stop the unraveling, in every way.

"I don't know what to think, what to say, how to manage this, because this is insane, of course. I longed for him all this time, yes, you know I did, but my longing was for the then Deke, not this Deke. I don't know this Deke. He's a complete stranger.

"Except..." and here, Fox broke down, "except... he smells the same. He smells like bees."

Rita imagined the thoughts in Fox's head: the good and the bad, the memories and grief, rearing Tate alone (well, with the help of four other mothers better equipped for the job than she and several father figures putting in their two cents, not to mention a superfluity of nuns), working day and night, thinking about Deke every minute.

And, yes, in an instant, just 24 hours ago, Fox's world turned upside down. Fox thought it was supposed to be like, "Oh, Deke's here! All's right with the world! It's right side up again! Let's get on with it!"

But it wasn't. She'd been missing a static Deke Harley, suspended in time. Thirteen years put miles on a person, even without a trauma to the head... but here we are.

It wasn't so much that he looked different, she didn't care, although he was certainly thicker, a bit softer. He'd lost his sharp edges, those sexy, sparkling parts that zapped the red hairs on her arms and made her legs like spaghetti. OK. She did care. Did that make her shallow?

"Dammit!"

She leaned over to the drawer. Her hair, prone to shock in electric situations, stood on end and flew around like coppery glitter.

She handed the old photo of Deke to Rita.

"You've had this all along?"

Fox nodded.

"You sly girl. We heard you got rid of everything."

"Not quite."

"So, what does it mean?"

"It means I missed someone who no longer exists. I missed the 25-year-old boy in that photo. I missed a ghost. In a way, Deke *is* dead. This is Deke, Interrupted."

Fox got up and walked to the window. It was dark outside, and her daughter and the newfound father were out there together, so happy. Probably connecting with Stevie right now, big reunion. Ho boy.

"Wouldn't you still love him if he'd been here these thirteen years? We all change, get older," Rita said.

Fox considered her sister's question. She peered out there into the night looking for the answer.

Why couldn't she be happy? Was there something wrong with her?

There was no answer for her sister's question.

"What do I do now, Rita? Tell me what to do."

How could her father invite the Harleys to stay at Sweet Farm without consulting her? She just might have other ideas, like some space!

And how long would they be staying? Were they assuming that Fox would welcome Deke back into her bed and her life and her daughter's life just like that? Snap! On a platter?

It was close to 10pm, and there was one more detail before this compound in Carmel Valley, now totaling twelve tired souls, could bed down. Rita shook her head and nodded at the same time, saying, "I don't know, but Poppy has picked up their mounds of luggage and all, so I think we should ask him."

Fox and Rita slipped out the deck door and around the Barn to the left, stopping by the Tea Room to pick up a cold Parmesan scone from the bin to quiet Fox's rumbling tummy.

They arrived at the door of their parents' bedroom, hot and bothered about his independent act.

Jock, the creator of this particular hash, was a bit taken aback, surprised by their vehemence. He ushered them into the room and the three sat down together on the love seats. Maria was ensconced in their bed with a book. She looked up over her tortoise shell half glasses, knowing what this was about. *Hasty Jock. Taking care of everyone.*

"Why, girls, I do apologize if this does not set well with the two of you," their father said. "I see your point, but can you truly think I would let members of our family stay in a hotel during a moment such as this? Today, those two people became responsibilities, family members: Deke Harley and his mother. They became pieces of our puzzle." Maria smiled at this, her phrase. He could thank her later.

"No, no, I do not think Deke Harley should be moved right into your bed, Fox. This won't happen," Jock continued.

"And, as to the unilateral decision, well, you were occupied, and Rebecca was getting nervous about the cab driver just sitting there in the parking lot staring at the door of the Tea Room, and I think she felt a need for a shower or a bath or a long sleep, I know I did, so the good host in me blurted out an invitation before my tired brain could catch up.

"I dispatched Felix and Chico to the hotel and put Rebecca down for a nap. What else could I do?

"No, I don't know how long they will be staying, but let's take it day by day. For good or bad, when you had that baby, and he was her father, marriage or no, he became our family, our concern. Do you see? Now that we know of it, his crisis is our concern. It remains to be seen whether or not he will be your man, oh, yes, I do understand you, my girl, I do. Don't look so surprised. But he is Tate's father."

Jock put his arms around his daughters.

"We can sort this out over time. For the moment, Rebecca is in Nana's room and Deke's baggage is in Jolene's. Let's leave it at that.

"And yes, my girls. Yes. I do think they should be here. With us. Yes."

Well, the Harleys were on the compound now, nothing Fox could do about that without being a total jerk. But, at least he wouldn't be in her bed or even on her couch. *Poppy's right. I know he is. They belong here. We can't sort out any of this by phone, or over dinner, taking tours of Cannery Row. Hello, would you like to come for cocktails at the Outrigger to discuss how we pick up off the floor all these broken bits of our lives?*

Deke Beds Down

Later, Deke, now in Jolene's yellow bed, was ready for a respite himself. He wasn't convinced this move to Sweet Farm was a good idea, either. Things were getting pretty complicated. The shift from the hotel happened without his knowledge while he and Fox were pretending to be half asleep on their former bed, so there was nothing he could do about it.

And there was *Sam*, Stevie. Just that alone gave him a headache. He had to think about *Sam*. Stevie.

What in blazes was that all about? Did she mean it, or was it a joke? The kid is fifteen years old! Oh, Lord! What if I had said yes? Not only is she underage by a mile and a half, she's my niece! Oh Lord. How did that happen? Or almost happen! Well, thankfully, fate intervened.

And there she was, tossing the contents of her stomach. She looked up and saw me there and threw up.

No, it was no joke. She meant every word.

Stevie's Sunday Morning

Stevie cried to think of her diminutive father out there in the kitchen making his familiar Soup of Consolation: the essence of chicken, the Fáno Michel cure for all ills. Perfect.

She could see him now: simmering tiny minced vegetables, blending this and that tiny thing sprung from his not-so-secret garden, sprinkling precious herbs, the not-so-secret-secrets of his bohemian French potions.

He poured his hand-crafted chicken stock, strained the plump chicken, cooled it, pulled each piece from the bone with delicate fingers. He poured his stock and he poured his love and he wrapped his arms around his daughter while he asked no questions and brought her Soup of Consolation, and she was comforted.

He had no idea.

Stevie let loose the pointing fingers on herself with a vengeance. Every nun in the world, every muse that ever blew in an artist's ear, every critic and every teacher and certainly every authority figure there ever was, stage-whispered his or her derision, bruising Stevie's already wounded pride and tortured soul.

After a cup of Fáno's soup, Stevie moved out to the Hobbit. She dressed in sweats and an old shirt of Fáno's and slipped barefooted out the sliding glass door onto the Chapel House deck. She dashed around to the little oak tree, up the three-slat ladder into her spot and curled up on the cushion, safely tucked away from the Deke Harleys of the world, not to mention every *Adam* of the Habsburgs with a dragon family crest.

There was nothing in the books she'd read that covered this situation: what to do if the man of your dreams turns out to be your uncle. And, what if you'd propositioned him to relieve you of your virginity, like some trollop, some pubescent hooker, trolling for experience? 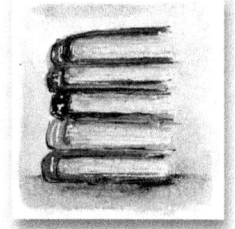 What would Betty Friedan have to say about this? Stevie's own thoughts were perhaps less eloquent than Betty's.

Whatever possessed you, Stefani Awena Michel, Sam? Whatever made you think you could go out into the world and ask some stranger to awaken you to the joys of intimacy? What absolute hubris! What cheek! What ridiculous folly!

The truth of this slapped her on the face right about the time she was throwing up.

First slap: Stupid fifteen-year-old girl with a 40-year-old stranger!

Second Slap: Worse than a stranger, her uncle!

Crapola.

And she'd have to talk to Farley sooner or later. She would hear Phoebe's rumbling motor in the driveway before too long if she didn't return his gazillion calls.

Just curling up in her little nest made her mind clearer. She'd call Farley in a bit. *A refuge is like a pair of strong arms around your shoulders*, she thought. She spread the knitted shawl over herself and settled back, listened to the rustle of oak leaves, bells tinkling in the breeze, the clacks of the bamboo chimes in the garden. The clackety-clack and the tinkling bells and the rustling oak leaves sang her a lullaby, sweetly crooning the young troubled girl to a half-sleep, a drifting, dreamy sleep, wherein the walls shifted and waved and the elvish began to move and speak.

Elvish, owing to its nature, writes itself in gold only and speaks softly, in silver-light tones. If you see elvish in colors other than the gilt that sparks its magic, beware!

Stevie, in her dreamy half-sleep, safe in the arms of the Hobbit House, saw the elvish on the wall re-form itself for her eyes alone. Elvish is like that: very particular on whom it bestows its wisdom.

> *Stay Bold, Don't let Go*
> *Stand Tall, Hear the Call*
> *Go with your Dreams, Say what you Mean*
> *Follow your Heart, Do your Part*
> *Mind the Gap, Lead the Pack*
> *Mend your Ways, Don't Delay*
> *Stay on Track, Don't look Back*
> *It will Flow, You will Know*

In her dreamy state, Stevie scribbled the Elvish to English translation in her journal. Then she dropped into a deep sleep, making up for hours missed during the long, dark and restless night wherein she wasted her profound imagination on worry.

When she woke, Stevie was surprised to find the translation in the journal. She thought she dreamed it: an elf, in a sparkly golden leotard and tights and one dangling earring wrote her a message in gold.

Fox's Sunday morning

In warm flannel pajamas, ironically grateful to be alone in her bed, Fox pondered the evening before and the evening before that. Was it only Friday morning she sat in the garden with a cup of tea idly thinking, *What if Deke Harley ever showed up?*

Oh, well. Deke had been on her mind first thing every morning for the entire thirteen years: the photo pulled from the drawer, a few self-indulgent tears. Something, every precious day.

And here he is.

I wanted this so much. I longed for this. Why aren't I happy?

Two nights in a row she hadn't slept. *This has got to stop. I'll be worthless soon without sleep. And, I've got to keep my mind in some semblance of order. Life goes on. Sweet Farm goes on.*

I should talk to Tate.

Fox fumbled around in her bedside drawer for the photo. She'd show it to Deke. No. Never mind. She put it back.

He was sleeping peacefully in Jolene's room on the other side of the compound, while she lay here in the same old empty bed, wide-awake, thinking about him.

She really didn't know what to think. This was a roller coaster. Since Friday evening about 5:30, she'd been up and down 100 times. She was nauseous from the ride: happy, sad, happy, mad, mystified, happy, sad, mad. It was all one, mixed together like a marble cake batter swirling around in her brain. A big hand squeezed her heart. The mystifying thing was not his being here. No. It was how she felt about his being here.

She looked at the photo. Why didn't she ever think he might have changed?

Pitiful, to think this picture and a bamboo back scratcher were all she had left of the old Deke.

That's not true!

She hopped off the bed, got down on her knees and pulled out the flat box from under the bed skirt. She rifled through the notions, knitting needles, odds and ends to find what she wanted, tossed it on the bed and pushed the box back into place.

Deke's Sunday morning

Deke was showered, dressed and sitting in the far corner of the Adobe House garden at the little red table under a Japanese maple tree painted autumn-red by nature. Deke's tender eyes preferred the shade and still, quiet corners. This spot offered a panoramic view of Sweet Farm and beyond. Over the low gate and fence to the right he could see the Hobbit House in its little tree - he heard something about this tree house from Tate last night, but he was not to go there unescorted. Or was that, ever?

He had a peek of the Chapel House, its pale paint glinting in the sun.

He panned his eyes left to the Barn, visible through the trees. He saw the fall garden on the Barn's west side, by the distillery —maybe tomatoes, and some late lettuces.

And this garden, in front of the Adobe, where the two-foot apricot trees he, Deke, planted in 1948, were now fifteen feet tall with a few fall fruits still clinging to the branches. Ha! And the redwood bench he made for Mrs. Jock's birthday in 1949 nestled in overgrown yarrow over there. The gate was new, with bright hinges.

Around it all: row upon row of lavender, trimmed back in neat mounds, like little cloche hats. Everywhere. Beyond: a few fields, Schulte Road, the bridge, Saddle Mountain, the Las Padres Forest. The bobcats, the big cats, the occasional bear deeper in the forest, the coons, the deer. Yelping coyote pups. Lupine and California poppies painting the hillsides blue and gold.

He remembered walking down to the Schulte Road Bridge once with Jock and trekking up the river to where the big frog catch had been for those Steinbeck characters. Jock was in his 60s then, and Deke could hardly keep up with him. Look at Jock now! Still in better shape than Deke, easy these days.

Deke breathed in his history, caught the scent of Sweet Farm—the clean, sleepy smell, the earth and herbs and oils. Paraffin. Paint. And lavender. Always the lavender.

In Deke's mind, a slide show of memories: Fáno up on a cart, pressing lavender flowers into the steaming vessel; the low rumble of the green John Deere tractor; the shush shush of the rake; Fox snapping a picture with a Polaroid, zip! Tate chirping, "De De-me!"

He saw Stevie as a baby in diapers and pink t-shirt with chocolate frosting on her round cheeks; Maria at the workbench pinning a quilt; Jock whistling the "Colonel Bogey March" as he hoisted bales of lavender on his shoulders to the Distillery.

These virtual snapshots ignited more in Deke's brain than anything had before this. Why? Why here? Four years, maybe less.

Perhaps it was because of love… the vividness of love, the brightness. It became the most important thing on earth - to regain that brightness, that beauty, once he knew he missed it. The four years here were more powerful, more potent than any time in his life. Before and after here, all struggle, all pain.

Here - here there was love. Had been love. Deke wasn't sure now what was left.

What did he expect? To gain it back in an instant? For most of the thirteen years, he didn't even know what he missed, so there was no real accounting for that.

Deke had no expectations. Just a hope. An idea. A flicker of a used-to-be thing.

The old Deke would have been up at the crack and getting on with the work, with goals and lists and major feats to accomplish: digging wells or building fences, tilling land. There were goals aplenty, and a girl to love at the end of the day. And then a baby to hold.

Today's Deke, the thirteen-years-later Deke, was pretty much free of goals, and absent of lists. He'd gone a little soft. Tate did not recognize the James Dean-ness of him because it was gone. All his rough edges had been sanded down, in the post-whack life he led on Snippet Sound with his mother and the Judge and Mrs. Judge and Great Uncle David, brother of the Judge. He even learned to play bridge, never Deke's big ambition, but, Uncle David was a mediocre bridge enthusiast and Deke was the obvious fill-in fourth. Chess was harder, but he could play alone. He checkmated himself regularly (Deke vs. Michael) and enjoyed every solitary moment of it. His were more low-key activities these days.

Deke sat at the table, listening to birds singing the morning awake. He heard the rustle of a robin or perhaps a squirrel in a bush by the fence. He watched a lizard dash across his shiny boot.

Deke's boots, the very footwear inspiring Stevie's dragon-based family crest during her 24-hour love affair with the imagined *Adam*, were his homage to his western roots, he'd ordered them by mail from a Colorado bootery. No self-respecting Marylander wore fancy cowboy boots. Deke didn't care. He was still and always busy putting one foot in front of the other, and the boots gave him hope, made him feel grounded.

He was well dressed, we can say that for him, for all his other problems. His jeans were new, his tan suede jacket soft and well fitting. His hair was shaggier: he combed it back wet every morning and for a while each day he had a debonair look, sleek and put-together, until the wind picked up all that hair and tossed it over his eyes.

He wondered, perhaps a little late, if he was wrong to come here, to stir things up for Fox and Tate and everyone. He should have called, maybe.

Oh, right. And what would he have said? "Hi ya, Foxie!" Hmmm. No. And she might not've answered a letter. Just showing up is better.

Should he admit he hired a snoop to find her? To make sure she wasn't married or moved away. He had only fragments of information in his addled head for the detective: Carmel, Flowers, Fox Wyman. That was enough. Carmel was no metropolis.

He stopped the detective work when he heard Fox was still in Carmel Valley, running the operation, as a matter of fact, and no, she was not married.

"Oh," said the sleuth. "And two more things. It's called Sweet Farm and they grow lavender."

Bingo.

He heard the gate squeak and looked up. There was Fox, head down, looking at something in her hand.

She hadn't changed, not like he had. Her hair was the same color, amber gold with coppery streaks. He noticed the flip at the end. She was lean. She was red. She wore her jeans and t-shirt as if born in them, meant for the outdoors. Did she know how well she looked? How beautiful? Probably not. Fox was never one for noticing.

If anything she was more determined, she'd grown into the job. His job. But, you could see it in her face and in the way she walked. Deke wondered again if she knew.

He coughed and her eyes flashed up. She stopped for a split second, and then continued, moving toward him at snail speed.

Fox felt herself moving in slow motion, like through waist-high water. She did not, could not look at Deke as she got closer, so she focused on his boots.

Fancy. Polished. She could see a tale etched in threads.

Fox couldn't imagine the old Deke wearing dragon cowboy boots. She wondered what other shoes he had. Back in the old days (would she be saying that all the time now?) he had one pair of boots to his name, scuffed high top Red Wings that serviced every need.

When she got to the table, she handed him his wallet.

"My wallet! Where was it? It wasn't stolen?"

Fox considered him for a moment. He looked so sincere. So amazingly innocent. And animated! That was refreshing. He was almost smiling.

"Apparently not." These were the first real words Fox had spoken to Deke since his arrival, other than, "C'mon," which she regretted once she realized she didn't know him from *Adam*.

"It was on the floor by the dresser in the bedroom. I found it the night you never came home."

Ah. That sounded better to Deke. Better than *the day you left*.

Stevie's Confession

Farley didn't ask why. The sound of Stevie's voice on the other end of the line was all he needed to hear - a taught rubber band.

Did he wonder what was stressing her? Not at all. It had to be about her Perfect Stranger. The only other drama currently playing at Sweet Farm was Deke Harley's return, but that was sort of Tate and Fox's business. So, it couldn't be that.

Well, he'd have to wait until he got to Sweet Farm, or perhaps even longer, if she wanted to go somewhere to talk.

He'd just finished his morning polish of Phoebe, his beautiful orange truck, when his mother called him to the phone. Now, on his way to gather Stevie up, he worried over her latest brilliant idea. But, it was Sunday, and IT was supposed to happen on Sunday, so perhaps they put IT off.

He arrived to find Stevie sitting on the Sweet Farm Rock at the end of the driveway, picking at the paint on the S. She drew blood from the cuticle on her thumb earlier, so she focused her nervous picking now on inanimate objects - paint on the rock, rust on the mailbox.

She looked a bit forlorn sitting there, Farley thought. Her braid was messy, like she hadn't brushed it out and re-braided it this morning. Like she'd slept in her clothes.

Stevie waved Farley over to the side of the road and hopped in.

"Where to?" asked her friend.

Stevie looked at him with sad and not-quite-cried-out eyes.

"Man, what happened, hon? You look terrible."

"Just take me somewhere. Anywhere. Where we can talk. I can't speak right now. Just… I don't care. Just go." She waved her hand in the general direction of *anywhere but here.*

Farley knew what to do. He handed Stevie a tissue and turned Phoebe around. At Carmel Valley Road, he headed west toward the beach. They rolled away through fields of golden grasses awaiting a fall rain. They passed La Casa Hay and Feed and then the Chuck Wagon Coffee Shop and he thought about a bacon burger with blue cheese, but Stevie didn't have any hungry look about her and the Chuch Wagon surely wasn't private enough for this conversation, he guessed. They'd run into everyone she knew in the Valley, so he passed up his favorite burger place and kept on moving.

At Highway One, he kept to the south of downtown Carmel, "the back way" Stevie called it, up Rio Road and around by the Carmel Mission and left down Santa Lucia to Scenic, the long snaking road along the beach, where he parked Phoebe in the shade, turned off the engine, got out of the truck and went around to the passenger door, which he opened wide and then leaned on the window with his right arm. Stevie sat perfectly still, looking straight ahead into some other world.

Farley said, "Steve."

Stevie looked up. "Oh. Right. Sorry." She noticed where they were, her favorite place. "Thanks. Good idea," she said. "Let's go there."

Farley took her by the arm and walked the forty steps to Stevie's special bench, at the south end of Main Beach with the Frank Lloyd Wright house to the left and piles of kelp pushed up against the rock wall and spreading across the beach below. She was used to the smell, pungent and sharp, musky seaweed and oxidized, decomposing ocean floor; it left this idyllic little bench to the intrepid locals, to Stevie. On her beach walks, Stevie sat here in reverence for the ocean, for the variants of the color blue, for the smell of kelp and the salty sting in her eyes.

The sting in her eyes today was of another nature. She sat quietly for a moment, looking out to sea, feeling smaller than usual, foolish and young and maybe manic - her imagination knew few bounds. She was, in fact, a little shaky still, even though her nap had calmed her heart rate, and when she turned to Farley and said, "I am a complete and perfect fool," her voice cracked and her eyes filled with the tears not yet cried.

He waited for more. This was Stevie Michel. There was always more.

She couldn't look at him, she focused her eyes on a fishing boat, a dot on the ocean-scape, but once she started, she threw caution and secrecy and humiliation to the wind, for she had to unburden herself of this beautiful turned ugly wreckage of her life. She wanted him to make it ok, to say she was not an idiot, a bad person, a Perfect Fool for the Perfect Stranger. That they were still friends. That he wasn't completely disappointed in her.

Oh, she told him everything. Well, she left out the part about the mysterious elf's message for the moment, but she started at the beginning, from when she saw the Perfect Stranger through the window at the Outrigger and gathered her courage to go in and talk to him. She told him how she sat right down and said, "May I join you?" like any woman on the make in a bar. She described ordering a lemonade (a lemonade!) and then proposing her de-floweration to him, straight out, like it was written in a script, and she played the part perfectly. She told Farley everything they said and about her next 24 hours, the party of love inside her head.

All of it, yep, because she knew she must, he needed to understand how forward she had put herself, and then he would get how low she was at this moment.

Lower than a snake's belly.

Lower than dirt.

Lower than worms.

She laid it all out there, even small details of Deke's arrival, which Farley thought was a bit off track, but he did not stop her flow. She was on a roll.

What a storyteller she is, he thought. *An amazing talent for stories.*

He was *with* her when she went to the kitchen after their phone call, when she made herself a PB&J. He could just *see* her sitting down to the counter with her milk in one hand and taking a bite of bread and jam. And he was freaked out for her when the door opened! Shocked, wondering if it could really be the Perf….

"Deke Harley? Is the Perfect Stranger? Oh, Lord. Oh no!

"Oh, Stevie."

Jock Pays Deke a Visit

Jock came to see Deke in Jolene's room on Sunday afternoon. The door was open, Deke perched on the little chair in the corner, laboriously writing in a notebook in pencil.

"You can come out, you know, Deke. You don't have to hide out in here."

Deke looked up and laughed. "Well, you certainly pegged me there, Jock. I am kind of hiding out.

"I don't how I'll ever thank you for taking us into the family like this, Jock. I didn't expect it. I don't know what I expected, but not this. Is it too hard on Fox? She's pretty jumpy with the whole business, I don't blame her, if she is. I sat in the garden for a while this morning, but I figure Fox doesn't want to see me around every corner, so for now, I have plenty to keep me busy. Doctor's orders, and mother's, of course, to write every day."

"Deke, you and your mother are welcome here. It's a big place, plenty of space for all of us. Fox needs time. Lots of time. This is the most shocking thing for her, your reappearance. She's in her fox hole, you might remember this."

"Ha. I do, now you mention it. She used to do it in the Barn, when she was mad at me but we couldn't avoid being in the same room! It was a combination of the silent treatment and that game we used to play with Tate: she would put her hands over her own eyes and think we couldn't see her."

"Yes. That's right."

"Jock, I don't expect her to take me back. I know it's not that simple. Oh, I appreciate the opportunity to stay here with you, for more reasons than being near Fox and Tate. More than you know. And, now I'm here, I have rushes of memories, a flood. Not just about being at Sweet Farm, but before, too: the Army, Cimarron County, driving my blue bike to Salinas from Oklahoma. It's kind of exhausting, so I am content to sit here and just absorb it.

"Poor Fox. I remember something I wrote in my letters to her about waking up in the hospital and seeing my mother's face and knowing her, really knowing she was truly my mother and not the woman who said she was my mother, sitting there beside me. I said in the letter, 'She wanted her son back, and look what she got.'

"Well, don't you think Fox is saying, 'Who the Sam Hill is this guy?' I know I'm not the man she fell in love with back then, but I am not a bad man, and mostly I'm just slower. With more padding. And maybe more patience."

"Not negative attributes," said Jock.

"No, well, I've had a lot of time to think. Too much time. We, that is, my mother and I, had no plan to move in on you, or make it hard for Fox. We wanted to make contact, that's all."

"I understand."

"Was it the right thing to do? There was no less shocking way we could think of to do it, except maybe writing to her first, but I was afraid she wouldn't see me if I did that, and it took us three years to figure out how we should make it happen."

"Absolutely the right thing to do, whether you and Fox work it out or no. You are Tate's father, and she is sky high with happiness that you're here."

"Yes. Yes, I am glad of that. She was the first face I saw in my mind when I awoke from the dream of me. The phantom me. When I woke up, Tate's little curly blonde head hovered in my mind's eye: those big dark blue eyes, her voice in my ear.

"And you know what? Although I've said it took three years to find you all and plan getting here… it was about working up the courage."

"Then it is better, sir, to love whom one cannot have?"
"Probably better," Lancelot said. "Certainly safer."
- John Steinbeck
The Acts of King Arthur and His Noble Knights

Farley and Stevie at the Beach

Farley longed for a cigarette. However, as neither he nor Stevie smoked, or had cigarettes, it was an inconvenient thought.

He hardly ever wanted a cigarette. He had a few once, when his sister's boyfriend, Pete, offered him one at the Starlite Drive-In movie in Watsonville. Farley (four years younger than his sister, Karen, and seven years younger than Pete) was dispatched by his father, Judge Simpson, to chaperone the date. He had to take the cigarette. It was a matter of pride.

At the drive-in movie, he cranked down the right side window and hooked up the fat speaker on the window's edge. He then scrunched down in the right corner of the back seat of the '58 Chevy Impala, in the perfect spot for a view of *Psycho* on the huge outdoor screen. Karen leaned toward the left, toward Pete, widening Farley's view of the screen from the back seat.

Pete lit a cigarette and offered one to Farley. Karen was aghast, but laughed in that *I told you so* way when Farley coughed and choked.

Never say die, thought Farley, and kept on smoking while they watched the movie. He liked smoking, it gave him something to do during Anthony Perkins's breakdown and all that considerably messy knife business, rather than biting his nails or twisting his hair, but it wasn't worth doing as a regular habit so he resisted buying any. Besides, he was 12 at the time.

But he wanted one now.

In the moment, with his arm around Stevie, sitting on the bench, watching the waves crash onto the beach, he felt so powerless to help her. All he could do was hold her while she cried. It made him want to bite his nails. Is it a bad thing that a girl's tears make you want to have a smoke?

She's cried a stream of tears, he thought. *Girls do have a never-ending fountain in there.*

But Farley was grateful for the tears, too, because they allowed him to hold her. He could pretend for a few moments that she was his, he the man of her dreams, he to show her the beauty of love and all that goes with that surrender.

Although, truthfully, he knew little more than she about the subject; he thought they might learn together.

"Farley?"

He snapped out of dreamland.

"Yeah, hon?"

"Am I a complete idiot?"

Farley took his time. He considered all the ways he might answer this question. Over the past few days, he did call her an idiot in his mind, myriad times.

This was delicate. She had beaten herself up royally, so she didn't need him to say *I told you so*.

And, the truth was, he admired her ability to go out and get what she wanted in this world.

"No, darlin'. You're just a bold, curious person. You just did something that most girls would like to do but don't have the nerve for. It didn't work out, that's all."

"You make it sound simple."

"Well, it is, really. I mean, you didn't hurt anyone. You're just embarrassed. I'd say you're lucky you didn't go through with it and then find out he's your uncle. I'd say you dodged a bullet."

"Well, that's a point," she said, drying her eyes. Sniffing, she said, "But, I've been hearing about Deke Harley all my life, the mysterious amazing heartbreaker, Deke Harley. I should have known."

"Did you ever see a picture?"

"No. There wasn't one. But there were descriptions. I should have known, if I'm so able to *see* people. I should have asked his name, maybe. His real name."

"Well what are the odds? It is kinda funny you know…" Farley said. Stevie let her gaze move from the vastness of the ocean, wherein a few hours ago she wanted to plunge herself, and looked at Farley's face for the first time since she began unburdening this tale.

He was smiling! How could he be smiling at a time like this?

But he was no longer smiling, he had started to laugh in earnest. His Salinas cowboy-ish face lit up with laughter deep enough to bring out his dimples, an event not common to Farley's usual serious and studious demeanor.

Stevie was shocked at first, that he could be so cruel as to laugh at her shame. But, the unburdening had done its work, and her secret elfin message gave her hope, so Stevie felt a bit lighter, relieved, even.

Soon, she was almost laughing, too. There was still much to consider, she being Stevie Michel; she wasn't through for a long way excavating her feelings about the extraordinary almost-mess she'd made of everything in creation, but at least she could be real with Farley.

Stevie's Personal Thanksgiving

Farley, dear Farley, said the one thing she needed to hear. Not that she had dodged a bullet, or that she could have been hurt, but that it was brave, bold, he said.

It was, but it was not a safe place to assert one's boldness, she knew that now. There was much to consider about her many ideas. She thought, *Anne of Green Gables never had to cope with these modern issues!*

She still didn't know anything about sex, but she certainly endured and loved and hated the excitement provoked by thoughts and fantasies alone. *What sweet torture the real thing must be!*

She said his name over and over in her mind, to not think of him as *Adam*. Deke. Deke. Deke.

He was never *Adam*, *Adam* was made up, all in her mind, *Adam*, a dream, a story, something that three people on earth knew about and she fervently hoped never another living person ever would.

Tate Has a Father

For the first time in their lives, Stevie was uptight about something, uncomfortable in Tate's presence. Was she mad? Did she, Tate, do something wrong? Say something?

Life was weird enough right now without this, too. Tate couldn't imagine what the trouble might be, she wanted to talk to Stevie about all this - the flippity flop of feelings, the flutter in her heart, like panic, the hollowness of her mother's eyes, the memories surfacing from a gazillion years ago. There was so much to discuss. Stevie must know this!

And then, she flew by like a Sunday morning drive with Farley was more important than the fact that Tate has a father!

But after a couple of days, Stevie took her cousin's hand and said, "Let's go see your dad."

There was still some funny distance, but she was nice again, Tate thought, almost herself, and wanted to be together and hear everything.

For Stevie, there was much unresolved business. She could listen but she couldn't talk to Tate, *Oh Lord, no, no.* She couldn't talk to anyone but Farley, at least he was off-compound, and he did make sense, but she felt like a fool and saw how close she had come to disgracing herself royally within the family.

She still thought the idea of the separation of sex and love had merit, and she had not let go of the idea that it was her body and her choice of how to use it and with whom and that she would do the choosing carefully, but she thought perhaps there was a better way to go about it than accosting a Perfect Stranger in a bar. Who knew who that stranger might be?

Maybe I was lucky it was Deke. I could be dead in a motel room.

They knocked on the door and Tate went in, Stevie a few steps behind. Deke was pleasantly surprised, although this was lost on Stevie, whose nervousness increased with every step, and she looked everywhere but into his eyes.

Maybe he won't recognize me. I could cut off my braid real quick...

Deke sat in the glazed chintz chair with his feet up on the little matching ottoman in the corner of Jolene's bedroom. He was Gulliver in a Lilliputian environment: small room, single yellow-quilted bed, small furniture. Not to mention the decor, which we only touched on while Rebecca was napping earlier, so preoccupied were we with the rapprochement of the two lovers.

The ceiling we remember: stunning half sun, half moon and stars, light blue sky on the sun side, deep as midnight behind the moon and stars. On the walls loomed a jungle of oversized leaves: split philodendron, Hostas, fruit trees and oak and eucalyptus, surrounded by low growing flowers and herbs: lavender, cineraria, daisies and bougainvillea. A fox peeked out, some chickens scratched on the ground, Misty the Beagle lay under an oak. It was not a particularly restful room.

Deke perched on the furniture like a swan on the end of a willow branch. His feet hung over the edge of the bed and his head bumped the wall. The chair was made for a dollhouse, he thought.

But he was used to funny furniture. His grandparents, the Judge and Mrs. Judge, their house was full of fragile antiques not meant to be sat upon, and certainly not meant for someone the nature and size of Deke Harley. His 6'2" frame cast a big shadow.

But, he gazed out the window and was happy. In his new life, life after IT, IT being the occasion of waking up in a field with a damaged noggin, he looked at things differently than in days of old. Now, he had time to sit and think, or not think, as it goes. One might have called it meditation, but Deke did not think of meditating. He just sat.

But in sitting, he naturally checked in with his higher self. He wasn't really conscious of it in that way, he just thought about things, and, especially in the last three years since his "awakening," he saw things. We won't call him a bodhisattva, or an enlightened being, but let's just say that Deke lost some of his vitality but gained a heart.

He loved Fox before, but he treated it casually, took it for granted. He remembered thinking in 1947 that because one day soon he would have to leave to go make arrangements for his mother, he would be freer to go if he didn't marry Fox. Other regrettable moments popped up, but that was number one. If he could, he would make it up to Fox and marry her now. Be a good husband. A good guy. A decent dad.

He looked up as Tate knocked and she and Stevie came in. He wanted to smile, but kept his face immobile. Stevie looked at her shoes. Is it just the Wyman women, or do all people study their shoes in embarrassed situations?

Our intrepid Stevie, however, was determined to overcome her *faux pas*, her false step, indeed. She was ready. She stood tall—call it erect in her case—for tall she would never be. She all but squared her shoulders, which she would soon adopt after observing her Uncle Deke and the new Great Aunt Rebecca move their bodies in that purposeful way.

Deke stood up as Stevie, brave girl, took the two steps across the room and put out her hand.

"Hello, Uncle Deke. Long time no see."

Well, he couldn't help himself now. He smiled wide at Stevie and simply said, "Yes, Stevie. Long time no see."

Almost immediately, Tate said, "Stay and talk to Deke while I get my guitar. I'll be right back."

Out the door she went. Whoosh! Stevie whirled around to see the disappearing back of Tate as she flew out of the room. Stevie was stunned, about to bolt in true Wyman women fashion, but she heard Farley's words, *Never say die!*

She once again boldly climbed the diving board ladder and dove right into the deep end. She looked at Deke, trying not to think of him as *Adam*. She had to take advantage of the moment. It might not come again for eons.

"Were you going to come?"

"No, honey, I made up my mind not to about one minute after I got out of that squeaky leather seat in the bar."

"I thought so."

"Why did you think so?"

"Oh, please, you would have been a cad to accept, now I think about it. Even if you weren't my uncle." Her face turned a lovely shade of beet.

"Aren't you glad? Considering?"

"Well, yes, of course. I… I actually want to apologize."

"Oh, Lord. For what?"

"Putting you in this position."

"It's no position. Nothing happened. It was just something on your mind. It's OK. I am in no position, believe me. I'm fine. I'd say you must be a might confused though."

"Understatement."

"Yeah. Well, don't worry. I'll never say anything. It's our secret."

"It's not that, Uncle Deke," she said, although she did breathe an internal sigh of relief. "I mean, before I knew you were Uncle Deke, when you were *Adam*, for that half an hour? And those hours after, while I waited for something to happen? I couldn't get you out of my mind. I thought I was falling in love with you. It made me mad, because the idea was to have this experience without getting love involved."

"Oh, whoa, now, darlin'…"

"No. Let me finish. I've been holding this in and it's got to be said or I'll burst, like an overripe cantaloupe. There's not much time, so just listen. I'll be quick about it.

"It was a mistake, for me to do that, Deke, and my friend, Farley, was relieved to hear, whatever the reason, that it didn't happen. He was worried from the beginning about my plan. He... he actually laughed when I told him it was you and what happened. That did make me feel a bit better in a weird sort of way. Farley says I was lucky it was you and that it didn't work out. He's right. I just... I just can't tell you how stupid I feel right now. I've had a bit of time to think about it, and... I was really... I was really full of it. I let my imagination go, like runaway horses. It's not the first time, but, pardon the rhyming, it's the worst time."

Deke thought a lot about *Sam's* "proposal," before and after he knew it was Stevie. He figured the girl, *Sam*, to be years younger than he and underage. He thought it an amusing and interesting proposal at first, being a lusty guy in his weakly remembered past, but Deke had not recently fallen off that turnip truck, and he hadn't spent all those years in unconscious contemplation of his navel to get involved with a young innocent girl.

He hadn't thought for a minute it could be anyone he knew, he'd been gone for so long, but to have this beautiful young gutsy girl turn out to be his niece? Suddenly it wasn't just about her being underage, he felt protective of her. She was his kin. He was protective of his kin. If he knew they existed.

He considered her young earnest face for a moment. He intended to take her very seriously.

"I think it's hard to make sex truly beautiful without the love, *Sam*. Pure lust is powerful, but not necessarily beautiful. You'll know that, when you get there."

Stevie smiled at their now private nicknames. Very private. She didn't think she'd ever utter the name *Adam* again in her lifetime. But she took this in. "Was Fox your beautiful experience?"

"Yes, it was. And, you know I never would've left her, if I had more than half a brain and an ounce of memory after that day. We had something sweet, sparkly, all kinda firecrackers and sharp, soft and fuzzy, all at once. We couldn't stay away from each other, no matter how crazy and reckless it was. And we were friends. And then Tatie popped into the picture, and... well, it was like frosting on the most beautiful and delicious cake in the world."

At that, Tate reappeared in the door and the moment was captured in a frame, set in place, and then their story moved onto the next scene.

Tate filled the room's space with music and songs. As she sang and played chords, Deke sat back in the little yellow chair and considered his talented daughter, Tatie, a miracle. He imagined the little girl growing over the years into this marvelous being. He longed to know every detail of her days and weeks and months, and perhaps some of that would come out over time, but he felt a satisfaction like a sigh, just being here, now, in this little yellow jungle room.

Tate worried that if she took her eyes off her father he might disappear in a puff of smoke. He might be a mirage, a dream. But, no. Here he is. This is not a dream, but the real live man.

Stevie meandered through all kinds of emotional forests, wondering how the fates had brought her into contact with her uncle on Cannery Row only to step in before the meeting went awry. She marveled at the feelings generated in her mind and body over those 24 hours and wondered which came first? Was it all in her mind? She thanked the fates, and Farley, too, for basically saving her life. Just for a moment she imagined how she would feel if she found out *Adam* was her uncle *after* he introduced her to, as Farley might say, the wonders of nooky.

Thank all the gods of all religions he's not an ass but a really nice guy, Stevie thought. *Having an uncle might be better than the Awakener of all Joy. At least for now.*

Certainly safer.

Dear Jo,

By now you've heard of Deke Harley's return. You'd think this would be family gossip too juicy for Stevie to deny herself the pleasure of telling you all about, but she says for me to write to you first, since it is my dad, after all, who's come home.

It is wonderful and truly weird all at once. He is changed, although I don't really remember what he looked like. Today I saw a picture of him my mother secretly kept when she torched the rest thirteen years ago. He was handsome and muscular. I always thought of him as kind of jagged and energetic. Actually, he was a bit like James Dean, so I feel better about my private little daydreams of him.

I don't remember what he was like as a person, but his voice is familiar: it reminds me of things he said and pointed to in the night sky back then.

He smells just the same, and it still makes me cry. English Leather.

Now he's gentle and kind of quiet. He stammers a little when he gets upset or when he's asked a question he can't quite grab the answer to. He talks slower, is slower than I thought he'd be, not dumb, he's really smart, but… just careful with everything, but that's from the brain injury. Not the kind of person you'd expect to buzz around on a blue Indian Chief. Thicker. But, beautiful.

His face is clear, and when he smiles, you can see the old Deke, he lights up, but he doesn't smile a lot.

I can't imagine him in black leather and jeans. He's all spiffy now: new jeans, suede jacket, polished boots.

I am still learning the details. They figure it happened somewhere around the Rodeo grounds parking lot in Salinas and he got dumped in King City: they found the truck in a ravine, but because his memory was missing and he wandered off and didn't have his wallet and used this other name he thought might be his, the police didn't find him. Sounds simplified here, but I know it's not.

Anyway, he's staying here right now, and so is his mother, Rebecca. My new grandmother. Now that is really out-of-the-park weird. She's nice, kind of old fashioned, speaks so softly sometimes you can hardly hear her voice. Mama Maria says she's "genteel," but when I looked it up, I thought it applied better to your Grand Mama Charlotte, being a Lady. My grandmother Rebecca is more throwback southern plantation refined, white gloves and drawl and all.

This will be hard for you to imagine, but my mother isn't exactly glad to see Deke. Oh, she's happy he's alive, but…

I understand. Thirteen years is a long time. Fox is PO'd because she knew he was alive and just wanted him to come home and now he is and he might as well be from Pluto. So, it's a happy/sad thing, you know? Who knows where it will all be when you come here for Christmas. He's in your bed.

I am glad you're coming. Stevie's been in the oddest mood these weeks, and I really am worried about her. She's been spending too much time alone in her room. Maybe your visit will pull her out of this dump she's in. I don't know.

Can't wait to see you.

Love, Tate

Before Thanksgiving

Deke offered to help Fox on the Farm, but that was out of the question. She politely turned him down.

He asked to her to go for a walk on the beach. She said, "Maybe, in a few days."

He said, "Will you ever talk to me?"

She gave him a simple, "Yes," and left it at that.

He filled his time in Jock's little den, making friends with his former not-father-in-law; writing his notes; listening to Tate talk or sing or play music or just breathe; waiting for Fox to come out of her hidey-hole and see him.

And what was she doing?

Fox sat on the bed with her knees bent, holding the photo. She leaned against her pile of pillows, nestled into her four quilts. She felt mildly foolish not talking to her long lost not-husband, but she had nothing she could say at this moment.

Oh brother.

She functioned in a time warp, suspended, isolating herself to un-grieve the last thirteen years. She could not do it by talking with Deke. She could only do it alone, down her hole, the safe place she created all that time ago. A deft maneuver, hiding in a hole in plain sight. Very fox-ish.

Rita had tried getting Fox and Deke together, but Fox asked her sister to let go of it, give it some time, because when there are no words, there are no words and you can't force them through your mouth, because when you do they are all wrong and something bad comes out.

"Believe me," Fox said, when they took their seats in the Tea Room one afternoon. "I have looked at this thing every which way from Sunday and I am just plain not ready to sit and chat with Deke Harley. Whether or not Pop thinks they should be here, he can't push this river.

"It's fine he's here - they are here - and I won't make them feel uncomfortable. But make it clear, since you're such a lovely go-between, and I do thank you for that, that the next move is on my terms. Otherwise, I can't bear it.

"I can't run away anywhere, you know, so my internal retreat is quite necessary, you can see that, surely?"

Rita did. It didn't change her feelings, but then, this was not her drama.

Rebecca and Deke were treated like family, welcomed into the gatherings without reservation. Fox, in fox fashion, kept herself occupied in the office, wherein she could avoid any confrontations during the day with either Deke or his mother.

It was just as bad looking into the face of Rebecca. Fox knew she wanted to talk, to be friends, but, like Deke, she'd just have to wait.

At night the sheer number of Wymans, offspring and companions filled the Middle and kept the conversation general during their dinner hour, but, anyway, Fox found many excuses to eat scrambled eggs and toast in the Barn and avoid them altogether.

In the Adobe House kitchen, Rita and Fáno began hearty food preparation for Thanksgiving Dinner. Chico pulled carrots and potatoes out of the cottage patch and gathered flowers from around the farm.

In the kitchen, the usually reserved Felix, eyes big with excitement, touched Fáno on the arm and motioned him out the back door for a chat. Shy Felix, he whispered in his friend's ear and Fáno's eyes widened, as if hearing extraordinary news. He went back to the kitchen door and whispered to Rita to come join them. She, too, made a little ho! sound, surprise mixed with interest. She joined the conversation and, as Stevie passed by the back door on the way to the powder room, she heard Rita say, "We'll have to check it out with Fox. No more surprises."

Stevie waited for Rita by the back door, but no information came from that source. Stevie gave her mother that *I know you know something, tell me now!* look.

But Rita calmly said, "It's OK, Sweetie. Tomorrow is soon enough."

Soon enough for what? Stevie wanted to ask, but her mother was back in the kitchen surrounded by the population of Sweet Farm, with no opportunity for further discussion.

What, now, did they have to clear with Fox? Curious.

Thanksgiving

After all those years in a shed on a dust farm, and then in a rattletrap trailer next to the dust farm, and more years before and after on Snippet Sound in a 300-year-old house with tiny slanted rooms, Sweet Farm and the Adobe House was Rebecca's Paradise. She gathered flowers and berries and owl feathers, following Chico around the farm on a treasure hunt. The food would fight for space around this growing table-scape, but Rita didn't mind. She enjoyed watching the taciturn Rebecca Harley emerge from her shell, holding hands with the chatty yet grave little Chico.

Stevic, the budding baker, made two pumpkin pies, all the while just dying to know what Felix and Fáno were up to out there. As she baked off the sugar pie pumpkins and dug out the tender innards, she pondered the situation. While rolling out the pastry dough, she was surprised that Rita and Juana had no demands on Felix and Fáno's time this Thanksgiving morning - they were wrapped up in some divergent project. *What? What could it be?* Ooh, it irritated her to be left out.

After consulting Fox, Felix and Fáno got to work. Fox agreed to the nice gesture, once she got over her initial reaction to the whole business. But she wanted nothing to do with it and didn't want to be present for the event.

The food was prepped, the turkey roasting, and the center-piece, which survived on that table almost until Christmas, was a work of art: roses and candles, tiny pumpkins and leaves, twigs, branches, acorns, late hanging fruit, feathers. Chico borrowed the Wyman's Polaroid Instant Camera to zip several grainy but treasured photos.

All Wymans and guests slouched in the chairs and love seats around the Middle or had disappeared for naps.

The aromas wafting down the hall from the kitchen brought Deke out of the little yellow room with vivid pictures of Thanksgivings of years ago on this farm flashing in his mind. The pies. The soup. The turkey roasting with lavender.

He thought of Mildred, the ancient cook at Snippet Sound, what she would think of lavender on a turkey ("You gotta be kiddin' me, Mr. Michael!"), when he bumped into Fáno in the middle of the Middle.

Fáno, not prone to exuberant expressions or very excited declarations, could not contain his enthusiasm. His dimples danced in his face. His black curls bobbed as he nodded his head to keep hold of his tongue for the moment.

He and Felix had finished their business and arrived at the Adobe to get together with Deke before they sat down to table.

Fáno looked up at Deke, a foot taller than himself. "Deke, *mon ami*, do you have ze moment?"

Deke was surprised, mostly by the "mon ami." Not that he didn't feel welcomed by Rita and Fáno. They were the most open-armed of all, but Fáno had never before accompanied Deke's name with "my friend" in any language. It did Deke worlds of good, just that alone.

"Yes, of course. I have nothing but moments." He smiled at his own self-deprecating jest.

"Come weeth me then, Felix has something for you."

Fáno took Deke by the arm to the front sliding glass door. "Close you eyes, pleez," Fáno said as they reached the door. "Ok, step to just here. That is right. Now, open."

"Oh! Fáno. Felix. Where? How? Where did this come from? Oh my word, I … Oh my."

And there he went, crying again. But, wouldn't you cry? For there before his eyes was the 1940 blue Indian Chief.

Deke wiped his eyes on his sleeve and approached the bike, circling. "Where did you get this?" he asked in the general direction of Felix and Fáno. It was a wonder!

"Deke, many years ago, I gave theez bike to Felix and said, 'Make theez go away, eet hurts Fox's eyes to see eet.' He did not make eet go far - just under a blanket in a shed behind his and Juana's leetle cottage. Right here. At Sweet Farm. All theez time."

Deke looked at the bike and then at Felix. "All this time, you kept it for me."

"Si, Deke. Yes, I knew if you ever did come back, you would want this bike."

For a family full of talkers, it's amazing how often they can be rendered speechless. With tears in his eyes, Deke grabbed both men and hugged them.

Those witnessing this presentation, Rita, Juana, the girls and Jock (Fox joined Maria in the master bedroom for a little chat and Rebecca had not emerged from her nap), wiped their eyes on their sleeves and left the men to it. Even Stevie, who loved all dramatic happenings in her purview. They wondered what Fox thought about it, but they saw the look on Deke's face, and that was all that mattered. Chico, Polaroid still in hand, snapped a beautiful shot that would one day make him famous.

"Can you fix it?" asked Felix.

Felix: quiet man, solid as steel, tenderhearted, but, usually, unemotional. His eyes, too, were filled with tears, because he knew what this bike meant to Deke as a young man, and, in his wisdom, thought perhaps it might give him something to think about while he was here, besides the silent Fox.

Smart guy, our Felix.

Rebecca and Tate

For all Tate knew, her Maryland family had owned slaves! Grandmother Rebecca certainly looked like a southern bred daughter of a Maryland Judge from an old plantation family of tobacco farmers: her big hats and long flowered dresses, the soft murmuring southern accent, the elegant gestures. She lifted her pinky when she held a teacup to her lips.

Tate invited her to take a walk down Schulte Road to the bridge and wondered what Rebecca would wear for a country stroll, but she had misjudged the woman there, too, for all her delicate dresses and hats. Tate had no idea Rebecca had lived 30 years in the Oklahoma Panhandle farming dust — this woman was no dainty spoiled daughter. She had grit.

Rebecca arrived at the appointed time wearing a loose dress, stout boots over socks and a floppy hat tied around her chin with a string.

"I've walked many a mile in these boots, and a dress doesn't hamper me much," Rebecca told her new granddaughter.

"That's OK," responded Tate. "Mama Maria says she doesn't know why anyone would exchange the comfort of "ze skirt for ze blue jeans!" She looked down at her legs and feet, the loose denims and comfy high-topped boots.

"You'll do fine," she said.

They walked to the bridge and beyond, all the way to Saddle Mountain and back, a good three-mile excursion to the end of the Schulte Road pavement and beyond, Rebecca never faltering. She and Tate kept up a good chatter along the way, in which Tate learned more about Deke, his past, his father Hiram's farming failures, his brother Hi's short life, Cimarron County, and everything Deke did before and after his four years at Sweet Farm. She learned about the trek on buses and trains across the country to find his people, the years in Maryland, the surgeries, the mysteries to be solved regarding Deke's lost time.

Rebecca and Tate sat on a log on the path up to the marching trees on top of the mountain. Tate told Rebecca about being fatherless and a bastard and about the weird alone feeling and about hoping and about putting all her hopes and fatherlessness and bastardy and aloneness into her music.

"So many of my lyrics are about my missing father. I'm sure Stevie gets tired of it. She hears it more than anyone."

"Have you played them for your father?"

"A couple. We're still shy."

"As well you should be. Fathers don't pop up just every day, do they?"

Tate smiled. "No, they sure don't. And new grandmothers, either."

Later that evening, Rebecca stopped Tate before she left the Adobe for her room in the Barn. She beckoned her to her own room, invited her in. Tate wondered where all the luggage went.

Rebecca went to the drawer by her bedside and took out a pouch. She held the pouch close to her chest, like a baby, tenderly. She said to Tate, "I've been thinking about this moment since Michael told us about you three years ago. I started loving you right then, when he let the cat out of the bag, and I wanted to do this ever since. My mother gave me these pearls when I went to Cimarron, and I never sold them, even when I hadn't a cent to my name, even

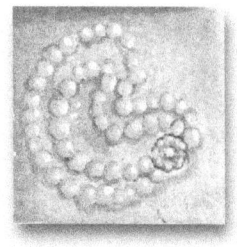

when we were eating pinto beans every night, because I knew I would have someone I wanted to give them to. And if I'd sold them, why, maybe we'd eat potatoes instead of beans for a few weeks, but the pearls would be gone.

"You may not want to wear them, they are a bit flashy," she said, unaware of the glitz factor in all of Tate's accessories, "but I want you to have them.

"My mother slipped these into my pocket, thinking they might change something, might save me from poverty or help me escape. But, I think if I had sold them, that would have been when I changed. They became symbolic to me, the pearlescent thread that held me to civilization. Even when I was alone, Hiram and Little Hi both dead, Michael off on some adventure: here, I suppose. When I was living in that little trailer, I would take the pearls out and look at them and remember Snippet Sound. I put them 'round my neck and thought of the girl, the deb, the delicate beauty, and it kept me going.

"Without your father, his letter to the Judge, his saving me at his own expense (he was on his way to slip that letter in the mail when he was stricken, you know) I would be dead by now, on my own, out there. So, I think we have saved each other.

"I leave Michael in your hands, my dear, he does need watching out for. Knowing he is with you for now makes it easier to go home to care for my mother. If he comes home to Snippet Sound, or if he stays here at Sweet Farm, I will love you. I want you to have these pearls, as a reminder of me, and your other family, whom you do not know."

"Whom I don't yet know. I will meet them someday. And, I thank you for these. I will cherish them. Put them on me, please?"

While Rebecca was fastening the diamond clasp at the back of her neck, Tate looked up and caught her grandmother's eye in the mirror. Tate said, "As to Deke," she smiled, "Michael. He is still my father, no matter what happens between him and my mother, so I think I can just let them figure it out and not worry about it. If he doesn't stay here, then at least I know where he is and where you are. That's something. More than I had before."

Fox and Tate

Before Fox knew it, Deke had been at Sweet Farm three weeks, and they still hadn't been in the same room alone or talked or even fully looked at each other.

Tate danced between her parents like a puppy, wanting so much to be all together. Tate was over her own angst regarding Deke's just showing up like that and, for that matter, his being gone for so danged long. She was just happy to have a father, this man, this father, who listened to her songs and constant guitar practice as if it were the soundtrack of his life - he couldn't get enough of it.

Tate sat on her practice stool in her tiny room, the Cube, she called it, with good reason. Roughly a 10 x 10 foot square, overflowing with Tate Wyman: her bed, her music, her books, her individuality strung along the wall: glittering accessories for her imagined outfits for the moment Tate and the Boys began in earnest, date to be determined. Sometime after Tate turned 21 in 1968.

Doodling songs kept her fingers nimble. She hummed in Spanish, a la Mama Maria, whose Spanish hums were legendary in the lavender fields. Humming in Spanish has its own flavor, an accent, an attitude.

She hummed in Spanish and doodled chords and picked out fanciful tunes while watching the sunlight make prisms of her belt buckles and ropes of rhinestone and crystal beads on the wall.

Fox appeared at the door, a rare occurrence. Theirs was not an easy relationship at the best of times. Not that this was the worst of times. It was pretty danged exciting and wonderful in the eyes of the sixteen-year-old Tate Wyman, whose wishes had come true. She felt sorry for her mother, who couldn't relax and let things just be what they were.

Fox said, "May I come in?"

"Of course, Mom. You hardly have to ask."

"I know. But, we… we usually don't…" Fox didn't quite know how to talk to Tate, not in any serious way. She stumbled over these next words.

"Tatie, can you see this is hard for me?"

Tate stopped playing her guitar and set it on the bed. She took off her headband and fine blonde hair spilled around her shoulders. She looked at her mother and tried to put herself in Fox's boots, but Tate had just surrendered to the joy of her father's return; she thought Fox was just being cold and stubborn, but she didn't say it. She wanted to say, "Lighten up Mom. It's a danged miracle!"

But she said, "Yeah, I know. But, it could be less hard. He's nice, you know. You haven't given him a chance."

Fox turned half away from the door to look out toward the living room window. Give him a chance. He had said that to her himself. "Fox, just give me a chance."

"I can't, not yet, Tate. Too much water has gone under the bridge. I have to get over losing him, get over my tears, the loneliness. I am not sixteen with a newfound father. I am a grown woman who's been through a personal hell."

"His life was hell, too."

"I know. But, can you expect me to bounce back like all this never happened? We are different people now, Tatie. I've gotten hard. He's grown soft. I can't explain it."

"It's OK, you don't have to. But, can you at least be happy for me? I don't want to feel guilty for being happy he's here, that he's alive!"

"Yes, I'm… yes, I am happy for that. But, I need time. Please, won't someone please just understand I cannot take this all in at once?"

Fox started to cry. She leaned against the door jam and pulled the ever-present hankie out of her pocket; these days she never knew when a flood might erupt from her red-rimmed eyes.

She thought perhaps she should move into the office, hide out there and just work 24 hours a day, she wasn't sleeping anyway, tell everyone to leave her alone and send her a sandwich every now and then. She had to be alone. What utter irony.

Tate examined her crying mother and wanted to shake her. But, no, dang it, she would just let her mother cry.

The Indian Chief

Deke and Felix sat on a log behind the cottage. Beside them was an open toolbox and in front of them, the blue bike, which they had just successfully started up. Vroom. Vroom.

With a great sense of accomplishment, even though it was a short-lived cough and sputter, they took a break to enjoy a cold lemonade and a moment in the shade of the little oak in the Rodriguez back yard.

It was a tiny, private space, protected all around by a high fence of thin slats. Juana's cutting garden still had a few blooms: late fall snapdragons, calendula, bachelor buttons. Chico built an elaborate farm scape in the dirt for his collection of little plastic barn and farm animals.

Deke could see clearly the line of Monterey Pines across the top of Saddle Mountain. It was a peaceful sight, familiar.

He leaned back against the tree and considered the Indian Chief.

"Thanks, Felix."

"For what?"

"For the bike. For keeping it. You could have sold it, kept the money. These bikes are worth a lot, you know. It's 23 years old and still runs."

"Oh, si, I suppose this is so. But, what do I need of money from someone else's bike? I thought you might be back, I did. And, if you never came back, sometime I would give it to Tate. It was fine where it was."

"Yes, I see. Well, I thank you, anyway."

"What will you do, Deke? Will you wait for Fox to come around? She's a stubborn woman, you know."

"Ah. Yes. She is. I don't know, Felix. I can't expect anything, really. I am biding my time. But, we'll see. I am grateful to be here, and to get to know Tate. Fox has every right to be stubborn. All those years, not knowing. I don't know if I can get her back, but I'm not ready to stop trying."

They were quiet for a few minutes, Deke focused on the pine trees, Felix with his mind on the next step.

"I have another idea, Deke. As you know, Juana, Chico and I leave in a few days for five weeks or so in Mexico. With little Jo and Nana coming, it might be tough on you over there at the Adobe. You could stay here, in the cottage."

*Excerpt from Stevie's Honors
English Journal 1963
TV and President John F. Kennedy's
Assassination*

On *November 22, the Friday before Thanksgiving, we watched the first programming on our new TV, for which we lobbied to watch Outer Limits and Dr. Who, What's My Line, The Lucy Show and Gunsmoke. We knew the Beatles were scheduled on the Ed Sullivan Show in February, 1964. We did not want to miss out.*

This journal entry was to extoll the virtues of our new TV, but as it turns out, it is more about President Kennedy's death and then everything leading up to the funeral. I mean everything. I have seen President Kennedy's brains splattered on the back of the convertible and on Mrs. Kennedy's pink suit more times than I can count. It's in black and white, but I know the suit was pink. I know the black and white color of blood. We are experts now on where the rifle was placed at the window, the ultra-composed features of the First Lady, what Lee Harvey Oswald ate for lunch. We watched the murder of Oswald on live national television by a man named Jack Ruby.

We gathered in Great Aunt Rebecca's room (Nana's room), where the new television was installed, generally the most neutral room on the compound, when we are not surrounded by new relations. Poor Aunt Rebecca. President Kennedy turned her private place into the most popular room in the house.

As I write this, I am gob smacked by the pure emotion wrenched from my 15-year-old troubled teenager's body while I watch all the gory details of a man's killing. Like I'm there, experiencing the trauma. I want to throw up.

I'm not so sure this TV thing is such a good idea after all. My president's death scene should be protected from a billion onlookers' cheap views. I hurt for Mrs. Kennedy, having to watch her husband die before the entire world while she scoops his brains off the back of the car.

Even Deke and Fox emerged from their respective caves to join the family for this awful spectacle. We are seeing history made. Poppy says, "We'll hear it for a long time: 'Where were you when President Kennedy was shot?'"

Now it is after Thanksgiving, after the funeral, President Kennedy has been put to rest beneath the eternal flame, and our TV is off. Time enough to see Outer Limits and Dr. Who, What's My Line, The Lucy Show and Gunsmoke. The television has lost its shine: presenter and televisor of bad news and trauma, which we get aplenty in our own natural lives.

Deke in the Cottage

Deke settled into the rocker on the Rodriguez family porch with the massive cat Gordo on his lap. The ancient rocker adapted to Deke's behind like an old slipper on a long-loved foot.

Felix, Juana and Chico finished the packing puzzle of their truck, now ready for a road trip, and walked up the path to the Adobe House to say goodbye to the Wymans.

In their absence, Deke watched two hawks catch the lift along the skyline above Saddle Mountain, hovering and dipping, hovering and dipping. All those years, just around the corner, just out of reach, this was what he longed for, never knowing, never quite grasping the "something" that waited for him. Those birds, right there. Those two birds.

Looking intently at the row of pines along the top of the mountain, he remembered a bus stop he traveled to by mistake on the road to Snippet Sound, a long time ago. He fell asleep and wound up in a town so small the bus stop was a closed gas station in the middle of Nowhere, Nebraska and they had arrived at 3am. The next bus going his direction would not be along for another two hours. Deke curled up at the back of the building within sight of the "Bus Stop," out of the wind. He fluffed his duffle bag pillow, in which he had collected a few belongings: a jacket, a pair of socks and a little kid's blue blankie he picked up at a rummage sale back there, wherever that church was... Denver?

In those early morning hours in Nebraska, shoulders incongruously covered in a mystery hand-me-down jacket and a blue baby blanket that reminded him of something, he just didn't know what, he dreamed. In the dream, he was up to his hips in thick molasses trying to get to a girl. She was all red…? She got further and further away. She waved. His movements were slow, he couldn't keep up with her. He kept pointing to his legs, to the molasses. When he tried to speak, nothing came out.

She ran to a line of pines, getting smaller and smaller. She slid under a blue baby blanket. She was a baby. She was in his arms. She was humming.

He shot awake to the sound of a beeping horn, right by his head. A bright light shined in his eyes. He sat up, afraid. He tried to keep hold of the dream, to remember it, but it flitted off, like a girl skipping away with her jump rope.

The bus had arrived and was honking him awake. He stuffed the blanket into the duffel bag, scrambled onto the bus and handed the driver his punchable ticket, hoping to go back to sleep to dream the dream again. He had to finish the dream.

But, it was gone. And he thought of it now for the first time.

He saw the girl: Fox. And he saw the baby. There were the pines. *The molasses must have been my brain*, he thought. The blanket? She still had the original. His eyes landed on it right away when Tate took him to see her jeweled belt collection. It clicked something in his mind at the time, but he couldn't grasp it. Now he did.

His new/old friend, Felix, came to the porch to shake his hand.

"Gracias, my friend, for staying with Gordo the cat, who is old, fat and very social, as you can see. Don't get up. The cat rules the lap in our household."

"Well, thanks for the place to be, Felix. It's like being at Sweet Farm but not."

"Si. That is right. It is why we have stayed so long on the Farm. It is our own little haven. We are not too much… in the way of each other.

"And Deke? Go slow, with yourself and with Fox. That is all I wish to say."

"Thanks, Felix. And I'll feed the chickens and all, you needn't worry about anything."

"Be well, mi amigo. Adios."

"Adios, Felix." He called to Juana and Chico, just opening the truck doors, "Adios, Juana! Chico! Feliz Navidad." They waved back.

Then they were gone. Deke rocked in the chair. Fifteen pounds of cat slept in his lap, but he didn't mind the rule. More reason to stay right here, rocking.

Deke and Fox had agreed to go slow (no worries there, Felix) but this was as slow as… well.

With his mother gone to Maryland, Deke felt a little vulnerable. He was used to Rebecca and her family watching out for him and he hadn't lived alone since 1946.

All the Wymans were right over the fence, though: Tate, of course, and Fox, if she ever cared to talk to him.

So far, she avoided him, but he caught her looking his way often when surrounded by Wymans and offspring. It amazed Deke how she could be down her foxhole in the middle of ten people. Just a look in her eyes. Not vacant: busy, involved, uninterruptible.

Later, Deke busied himself with his notes. He had a little box with a set of No. 2 pencils and a tiny eraser. This spiral notebook, his journal, was the third he filled with his small looping script since the first remembering, organized in little rows and columns: Memory, Date, Place, Details, Names. If he consulted his lists often enough, the words and pictures stayed in his head longer. He had a trail of dropped memories not written down, which made him cranky. But the list was getting longer and the memories bigger and better.

He wouldn't tell her, she would be spooked, but Deke thought the increased remembering was because of Fox. Being near her made him feel so alive. It made him itchy to do something. Besides sit.

Jolene and Nana Arrive

Jolene curled up in the back seat of the Fleetwood, Jock's cherished Cadillac, thinking about her dad, the dear departed Chuck.

Sometimes she heard his voice, especially in Grand Mama Charlotte's flat in London. There, it was the Super Conductor's voice, strong and assertive: she heard him shout, "Ta Da!" In California, it became a whisper, the Squashed Bug in her mother's words, but definitely still there, humming in the back of Jolene's mind. She hadn't explained it to anyone, but she did consider telling Tate and Stevie. No distinct words or messages. Just the sound of his voice. A hum. She'd gotten used to it.

But, if she told them about the humming, she might have to tell them about the secret. Which was in the imaginary box.

While her grandfather drove and her mother stared out the window in the front seat, Jolene remembered the night in Grand Mama's flat, after her imagined "box of secrets" ceremony. She worked herself into a tizzy trying to imagine away all the heartache and stress of keeping her father's secret these last three years, and in that frenzied fit, all in her head, she wrapped up the secrets in a tidy little imaginary package and was prepared to visit Bixby Bridge when she arrived in California.

She had imagined the cobwebby, wooly covering on the imagined box so well, it felt rough and heavy in her hands. She looked forward to tossing the whole shebang into the ocean.

And then something funny happened. Not something funny, ha ha. Something out of this world, mysterious funny.

Jolene was talking, well, ok, arguing with her mother, Nana, about the key. Not a new argument. The same as always. The *Why don't you get over trying to find what the stupid key opens and get on with your life?* argument. But this time, Jolene reached to touch the key hanging on a chain around Nana's neck, and it was hot! Jolene's hand flew back like the key was pushing her away. Her fingertips burned.

That was a new one. It made her stop and reconsider this whole key business. It was seriously hotter than her mother's body temperature. Like, sizzling.

When Nana asked her daughter what was wrong, Jolene simply stared at her mother. And, Nana was further surprised when Jolene stopped nagging her about the blessed key.

Jolene bumped along in the back seat of Jock's car moving south on Highway One, thinking about the Super Conductor. Each ride home from the Monterey Airport to Sweet Farm since Chuck's death had been the same: everyone thinking about Chuck, remembering other rides, Chuck incidents, but no one talking. It was like having him in the car.

Nana tried squeezing Chuck out of the car, but he just wouldn't go. He bothered her more in California, she felt taps on the shoulder, smelled gin breath, but she pretended all was well. In England, especially at home in Charlotte's flat, his presence was large but benign, like he was so very happy she spent all her free hours trying to fit the stupid key into some lock or other. Here, his presence was like a gnat. Agitated.

He controlled her from the grave.

She was afraid she was losing her mind. No matter what she did, she couldn't stop the chatter in her head. Nothing specific: like the sound of a hundred people trying to all talk at once over a telephone line.

At first she tried to zero in on one of the voices, but the headache from that concentrated effort wasn't worth the reward.

Which was nothing.

Jock tried small talk with his girls, but as they stretched over Carmel Hill and descended toward Carmel Valley Road, he finally gave up. He could hear the things they weren't saying.

From the back seat, Jolene finally asked about Deke.

"What is it like, having him home? Er, back, or whatever."

"Well, I'd say there are eleven answers to that question. And you and your mother will come up with two more. For me, it's an odd new friendship, with a new man. You never knew him, but he was different than you'll find him now. We weren't friends, just Boss and Worker for a while there, and then what we called *not-father-in-law* and *not-son-in-law*. It's complicated."

"I know what is it, Poppy. I'm fifteen, not a little girl."

Jock looked at his half-English granddaughter in the rear-view mirror. If she was mature at twelve, now she seemed like a grown up college girl.

"I know, honey. I'm sorry. It's still complicated. But, anyway, I like him. I root for him and Fox, but only the angels in the sky can tell you if they'll get back together. Your cousin Tate is deliriously happy. He is staying in the Rodriguez's cottage for these weeks you're here, which is brilliant. It's calmed down the farm, without Deke Harley in Fox's face every minute.

"As for the rest of it, my pet, you'll just have to see for yourself."

They turned right onto Schulte Road and right into the Sweet Farm driveway.

Deke and the Girls

Deke prepared a little lunch for Tate and her cousins. He layered cheese, pickles and thinly sliced onion onto bread buttered on both sides. The pan was hot and ready to grill his cheese sandwiches, and the only soup he knew how to make, Fresh Tomato a la Madge at Keebler's in King City, simmered on the stove.

He went out to the little herb garden and picked some fresh tarragon to sprinkle on his soup. He checked the time: five to twelve. He flipped the top pieces of bread onto the four sandwiches and placed them in the big pan to sizzle. He looked up just in time to see the three girls come in the gate.

He wiped his hands on the white bar towel hooked in his belt and went to the door to open it. Tate had her hand up, about to knock. She giggled and tapped him on the nose.

"Hi, De-De. It's me! And Stevie. And, look, here's Jolene."

"My mom says she's excited to see you at dinner tonight," chirped Jolene as she came through the door. "She didn't want to crash our lunch, but she sent you this: it's peanut brittle from this little candy shop in Piccadilly. She remembered you like it." Jolene put the candy box down on the little counter and took Deke's outstretched hand in both of hers.

As usual, Deke was touched to tears by both the peanut brittle and the hand grasp. He had wondered what he'd make of the British girls, and certainly what they would think of him, but he needn't have worried. He could see that now.

"Well. Welcome to my little temporary abode." He stirred his soup and wiped the tears on his sleeve. He flipped the sandwiches over in the pan, turned off the heat and let them brown for a minute while he properly greeted his guests.

When they sat down to the table with the soup, sandwiches and a little lettuce from Juana's garden, the conversation soon turned to Deke's story "…and how did you learn to make soup? This is delicious!"

"Ah, well, I was just thinking about that. I guess you might know about Madge, the baker at Keebler's, who was nice to me, let me work there and didn't ask questions. I was always happy when no one asked questions. The answers back then were hard to come by.

"But, anyway, this Madge, she answered my knock one morning, and I washed dishes for… I don't know how long, exactly. And I made soup. For a week, maybe? I thought I might like to go there sometime, to pay Madge back for the loaf of bread I took with me on the day I left."

"That was a long time go, Deke. Madge didn't keep track." Jolene was sure of this.

"Oh, maybe not," Deke said, "and I am not positive that was even her name, but I do remember Keebler's, and I know it's still there." He smiled, like it was a joke on himself. "I figure I owe her about a $100 by now for that loaf of bread." He looked at the girls, who had stopped slurping their soup and were staring at him. Tate was right. That smile was killer.

"What?" he asked. Tate and Jolene were speechless. But Stevie, who still avoided Deke's beautiful face, especially when he was smiling, looked out the window and, while keeping her eye on a chicken scratching in the dirt, jumped on an idea.

"We could take you."

"Take me where?"

"To Keebler's," she said to the chicken. "I know you don't drive, but Farley would drive us. His truck isn't big enough for five, but he could borrow his parents' car. Or Henry Pedigo's Edsel. We could go to Keebler's for lunch and you could ask about Madge."

Deke stared at Stevie. "You would do that?"

"Sure! Wouldn't we, girls?" Stevie took her eyes off the hen house and looked at her cousins. Everyone nodded.

"And just think, if Madge is still around," Tate was into it, "she could tell you how long you worked there!"

"Well, now that is an idea. Who is Farley, anyway? I've heard his name mentioned."

Before Stevie could speak, Tate said, "Farley is Stevie's best boyfriend who would do anything for her."

"He is not my boyfriend. He's a friend." Stevie blushed.

"He'd still do anything for you. You should know that. You're so dense sometimes."

Stevie took her eyes off the hen house and looked at Tate. She shook her head and said, "I'm not dense. I want him as a friend."

Christmas Eve Day

Deke arranged the contents of his considerable luggage on the picnic table and patio furniture in his temporary front yard. He made neat stacks and carefully covered it all with several sheets.

He once again expected guests: the entire Wyman Clan, nine people for coffee and a cinnamon cake Rita had baked for him earlier that morning. She also supplied the thermos, the cups and the coffee and arrived at party time with a bowl of fruit.

He was nervous. Even Fox was coming. He wasn't sure how she would take any of this, but he had recently stopped counting on whatever Fox would do or say. He realized she was as far away as Nova Scotia. If she would ever come to him it would not be soon. He decided to ignore her.

Instead he focused on his daughter, his memories and his future, with or without Fox. He had plenty to keep him busy. The Rodriguezes would be back in a month, and before that time, he wanted to know what he was going to do. He couldn't stay at the farm forever, obviously. No place for him here. Oh, sure, if Fox ever came around, there would be a place, but he couldn't count on that. He was just slower, not stupid.

When the party was gathered, Deke got ready to make his little speech. He tapped his cup with a spoon.

"You all have been good to me these last weeks. I'm not great at off-the-cuff speechifying, so I wrote your family a letter. Writing comes easier than quick wit these days." He dazzled his smile around the Wymans and Fox flinched in the light of it.

Dear Folks at Sweet Farm,

I know mine is a fantastic tale, and it surprises even me. Sometimes I don't believe it. But when I have one of my headaches, it seems real enough.

You all have grown and moved on, and I'm not sure of my place here, except I know for sure I'm Tate's dad.

When I had what my mama calls my cognitive epiphany, that is to say, when I woke up one day and remembered my girls, why, I began to think of all the birthdays I'd missed, all the Christmases. All the special days in a person's life. I started to put the pieces of my puzzle together and, like Mrs. Jock says, one piece leads to another.

That was when I started buying things. I based my purchases on what I could remember of you, and what I thought you might have become.

As he read the letter to the Wymans, Deke walked around the patio and uncovered the little piles. It looked like a market stall, sorted and stacked, beautifully displayed, artistic even.

This is for all of you, my gifts to you, collected over the last three years, to make up for the lost time. So much time lost.

A picture of the side porch at the house on Snippet Sound crammed with all this stuff came into Deke's mind. His grandfather, the Judge, said he was *buying love*. But, Deke didn't care. It gave him purpose.

He set his letter aside and picked up a box. "I used my intuition, and the little bits of memories. This fly-tying kit is for you, Jock. I remembered you like fishing.

"And this set of small tools is for Rita. You used to ask me to borrow the small hammer and such. I found this miniature set rolled in this cotton burrito with these little pockets and it made me think of you."

"And, Deke, these squares? Where did they come from?" Maria was running her fingers over the stacks and stacks of neatly cut 8 inch squares of fabric: beautiful cotton florals, soft, rich velvets, suede cloth, flannel, upholstery prints. She was practically purring.

Deke blushed, and said, "Mrs. Jock, I didn't have much to do in Maryland, my job was uncomplicated and the household work is handled by the staff, so my fingers itched to do something. I took some kidding for this, but I guess I could handle scissors when I couldn't hold a knife properly or I let the drill get away from me. Oh, I'm better now, but there was a time there I was downright useless.

"So, anyway, I cut those squares for you.

"And, I had no idea what you'd be reading, but I knew you all would be reading, so I collected books everywhere I went, too.

"And Tatie, this little part over here is for you. I knew you'd love music, you sang babbly tunes as a baby, and banged on anything that made a noise, so I found this fiddle for you: I didn't know why, but I thought you'd want to fiddle at the moon, and that made me remember the nights under the stars.

This portable record player is for you - it will play these LPs and 45s."

The extraordinary bounty covered every available surface: fabric, seeds, shawls, jewelry, beads, yarn, the fly-tying kit, many more small tools and sundry items for farm life. And books. Books of every description: novels, histories, biographies, children's stories, art books, cookbooks.

"You could open a store with all this, Deke!" said Jolene, and then covered her mouth, afraid she'd made a mistake.

Deke laughed. His gifts for Fox, he would save for later.

After all the thank yous were expressed and a good time was had by all, as the group began to leave through the gate in ones and twos, Tate asked her mother to stay after the others went about their business on the farm.

Tate Gives Her Parents the Word

"I want you to relieve me of the curse of bastardy." The three of them were alone now in the cottage.

"What?"

"I am sure you heard me, Mom. I want you to get married. I want to not be a bastard. I've waited all my life for two things: to see my father smile and to not be a bastard. I think you owe me this. Maybe I won't care about it someday, but today I do. It is all I want for Christmas. You can live however you want, but get married. Do this for me. Please."

And out the door she slipped, like an elf. All of a sudden, Tate was just gone.

Deke and Fox were left alone, looking everywhere but at each other. Thought bubbles crashed into each other, colliding in the minds of the two panic-stricken people. Fox was afraid Deke would ask her to marry him, and afraid he wouldn't. She so longed to be loved, but she couldn't find the path to it.

She looked at Deke. Deke looked at Fox with the intensity of a hungry bear. He scared the living daylights out of her. Well, he didn't scare her, exactly, but the situation did.

They blurted at the same time:

"We can't get married just for her," and, "She's right, you know. We owe her."

Their opposing views filled the cottage with unspoken words. A few seconds of that deadly silence was all he could bear.

Deke said. "Look, Foxie. I'll go away if you want me to. All I ask is that you think about it carefully before you say no."

"Think about it carefully? That's a laugh, Deke. What do you think I have been doing for these weeks, singing folk songs, sipping martinis?"

"No need to be hostile. I'm not the enemy."

"No, no, of course you're not. But, I have been thinking about it, and I understand everything Tate said. I am just not sure I can do anything to make her happy right now. I will not marry you for her, and I won't be rushed into anything. In fact, I am leaving."

"Leaving?"

"Yes. We are closed the next three weeks. I have the use of a cabin in Ben Lomond."

"I am forcing you out of your own home by being here. I should go."

"No, It's fine. You were right to come. I just need to be alone. I won't stand in Tate's way. I just want to get away from here. It's all I can think about. Let me go and I'll talk to you in a week. A week. Then, we'll talk. Just give me a week to… give me a week."

"Yes, sure, Fox. But, honestly, I'd be happy if we could just be friends."

Fox left the cottage with that on her mind. Friends. *Dammit. What does that even mean?*

The door to Tate's room in the apartment was closed when Fox wrestled herself free of Deke's hungry bear gaze and made it home, after the grudging promise to think about it, IT at this moment being Tate's request that her parents actually tie the knot.

Lord have mercy on my soul, Fox thought (in the vernacular of her mother church). *Dammit*, (in street-speak), *What do I do now? How much more of this can I possibly take? Get married! Is she kidding me? How can I marry someone I don't even know?*

While washing her face in the tiny bathroom sink, Fox received a clear message from her sisters. They were together, she could tell.

A few minutes later, Fox tapped on the door and walked in to Rita's little house. She slipped off her shoes and joined Rita and Nana sipping tea at the kitchen counter. A third cup had Fox's name written all over it. Rita was pouring.

"We thought you'd never get here. What was that all about?"

Unthinkable

Fox was doing the unthinkable. She had a seat in the front of the bus, right behind the driver. She'd never taken the bus anywhere in her life, except the school bus, and that was light years ago.

But the unthinkable part was not the bus at all. No.

She was on a bus going away for a whole week. By herself. Alone.

Unthinkable.

She surprised everyone. The folks on the farm encouraged Fox to take vacations, but she never did. She thought the farm would collapse without her. She knew better now.

Reasons #1 through 5 or 6: they were closed for the three weeks after Christmas; all orders were filled; the distillery was shut down while Felix and Juana were in Mexico; and she had no bookkeeping, no plan, and nothing to create.

Why shouldn't she take a vacation? So what if the theme was "To marry or not to marry Deke Harley." She was carrying that question around in her basket anyway, so why not just take the basket with her and think about it there.

She remembered the cabin: too crowded for four high school friends on a lark, but perfect for one confused not-wife whose illegitimate daughter needed a name.

Long walks in the woods. Feeding the fish in the pond. Sitting by the pond with a book. Sitting by the pond with no book. Who cares?

I can't even remember the last time I was alone. Maybe in the truck on the way to and back from the feed store.

The day after Christmas wasn't the best day to travel: sunny and hot for December; full bus, lots of kids, chattering, screaming, demanding. Two grandmothers swapped stories behind her, cackling about their ancient shenanigans, laughing at what their grandchildren didn't know about them.

The bus driver looked at Fox in his rearview mirror. "Going far?" he asked in a good-natured, friendly-bus-driver kind of way.

She looked out the window and said, "Depends on your point of view."

An Excursion

On a sunny December day, four exuberant teenagers and a fragile 40-year-old man piled into Henry Pedigo's shiny red Edsel convertible as Henry himself looked on. Henry's eyebrows were skillfully knitted together into one dark line, his brow puckering in a sorry attempt at a dignified frown. He watched as Farley rolled down the custom-made red convertible top.

"This is highly unusual," said Henry, jingling the change in the pocket of his perfectly creased jeans. "No one drives Isabel but me."

"It's OK, Henry, my pal. You know Izzy is in good hands. Who helped you put this engine in? Who crawled underneath and fixed the transmission drip with a bar of Fells Naphtha? And besides, I have left you with my illustrious Phoebe. There is no vehicle more… orange than she. She'll get you back to the school. She's just not big enough for this important expedition."

Lancelot couldn't have expressed it better. Stevie giggled.

"Hardly a pawn shop trade value," says Henry, watching Farley's hand stroke the Edsel's steering wheel and slide the key in the ignition. Henry waited for the familiar squeak upon start-up, but Farley's touch was smooth as glass.

"Hghmph," said Henry, mouth turned down. "How long'll you be? Going all the way to King City in my Isabel? You'll be gone for hours."

"Lunch and conversation, Henry. Three hours or so. We'll meet you at your house. Wish us luck! And try to wipe that smile off your face. Thanks for coming over."

Henry, frowning still, wondered why he was wishing them luck as they sped away, not just in his beautiful high-class "red-headed" car, but his cool ride back to his most excellent job teaching science and math at the Middle School. Henry rolled his eyes at the big orange truck, opened Phoebe's driver's side door, sighed all the breath out of his lungs, brushed imaginary crumbs off the seat and got in. He watched them: Farley, Stevie, Tate, Jolene and that fella, Deke something-or-other, tootling down the road away from the Simpson's hill.

Hghmph. They better be careful. No tellin' what they're up to now.

Solid Farley. Stevie's Lancelot. She observed his gift of persuasion in action there with the reluctant Henry Pedigo. She'd want Farley on her side for sure. HenPed was no pushover, and Farley had him wrapped around his finger.

Stevie chose to sit in the front seat, not to be next to her personal attorney-to-be, but to get as far away as she could from Deke's intoxicating aroma and still be in the car. *Thank God this is a convertible,* she thought as they sped along with the wind in their hair. *Whose idea was this anyway? Spending the whole day together! Oh! Mine!*

Deke squirmed in the back seat between Tate and Jolene, keeping his eye on Farley's driving. Farley looked like a safe enough driver, but all the way to King City meant, what? How long? He couldn't remember. Being dependent made his blood simmer.

The sound of the car and the rush of the air in their faces made conversation difficult, so Deke kept his eyes on road signs and the view, holding them in his mind for later, when he could write down the visions. He had no memory of getting to King City back then: he woke up nowhere with no name and pretty much nothing. *These hills along the highway just look like all the hills along all the highways in the country. We got oak trees here. We got the cows. We got horses. It all looks alike.*

Deke droned on like this inside his head for a few minutes, looking for something familiar to land on. Farley enjoyed the ride of the Edsel after the rocking horse action of the famous orange Phoebe.

Tate saw horses, and a cowboy hat blown off a rider's head, and the sun glinting on a spur on another rider's boot. Ooh, he's in some kind of round-up. With spurs!

Jolene squinted for the blur of colors: green and golden hills blended into blue sky then fuzzed into the shiny metallics of the cars whizzing by.

Stevie gazed on the rolling hills and floating houses and blurring colors and horses and cows and all the goings on as if it were the backdrop of her own personal movie: she filled it with extras and animals and all the things she'd need to have a beautiful life story. She imagined a soundtrack, something like Bach's Air on the G String, only with a piano arrangement. Her story would have piano.

Deke was an extra in her movie, now that he was no longer *Adam*. She'd have to find another leading man, a new prince, and no stranger this time. She'd get to know him and be just a regular girl.

She saw a row of mailboxes at the head of a dirt road. The sign said "Hackeysack Camp Grounds," crossed out. She thought "Amsterdamia" was scribbled over it in white paint, but they were moving too fast to be sure. She fantasized on a prince from Hagginsack County on the Isle of Hamsterdamia.

A few miles later they were in King City, parked in front Keebler's. Everyone in the car turned to look at Deke, a wordless, "Now what?"

Deke sat very still. It was simple. The memory was a back door and a kitchen. *Just go to the back door.*

Deke said, "How 'bout you all go in and get a table and order me something cold to drink? I'll be right along."

The four teenagers moved toward the front door as Deke lit a cigarette and walked around the corner. He stood in the shade for a moment, wondering what the Sam Hill he was doing with these kids in King City. What could come of this?

He meandered further and came to the back parking lot. He stubbed out his cigarette and threw it in an old rusted coffee can by the back door, full of the stubs of many a worker bee's 10-minute break at Keebler's Restaurant. He remembered the can there by the door.

The same door. There was the little hole in the screen right above the wood kickplate across the middle. There were names and initials scratched into it. He remembered the sound it made when it closed automatically: swoop and click. He thought of Madge, her curls escaping a net, her apron. The smell of bread.

He couldn't go any closer. He was definitely afraid, but didn't know why. He couldn't mobilize his legs.

Deke waited a few more minutes before he pushed his legs the other way and joined his young friends inside. He wiped his wet shaking hands on his pants and tried a second time to pick up his lemonade. He slipped a straw into the drink and pulled it to him across the table.

The kids (he couldn't help himself, they were kids…) the kids were talking about two friends they'd run into at the counter so they didn't notice his agitation as he sat down. But soon Stevie, daring a look at his face, said, "Uncle Deke, what's up? You look like you've seen a ghost."

"I don't know, I don't know," he said. "I'm just not too sure about this."

"What would you like to do? We're starving, should we order?"

"Yes, sure, go ahead. Just let me sit for a minute."

Blather and palaver ensued while the four teenagers decided what to have: burger, burger, tuna sandwich, patty melt, all with fries.

Deke's eyes wandered around the room. He didn't come out to the dining room but a couple of times back then. He remembered those swinging doors. Now he could see the feet of the person about to come out those doors from the kitchen. The feet were in red Keds and were attached to a pair of skinny legs, knobby knees exposed by a short skirt. Why did he recognize those knobby knees?

The woman with skinny legs and knobby knees and red Keds delivered a large tray of food to a group of construction workers on their lunch hour, burly men six to the booth squeezed together like plump oily fish in a can. She gave them extra napkins for their meatloaf and meatball sandwiches and turned toward Deke and his table of companions.

She set her tray on a service table and pulled the little notebook out of her apron pocket, took the orders: burger, burger, tuna, patty melt, and looked at Deke, waiting… he wasn't really hungry, but he needed something to do besides fidget. He said, "Please, I'll have a cheeseburger with no fries." He handed her the menu, looking up and into her face. She stared back with a shock of recognition, but she didn't know why. He looked out the window and frowned.

He wondered if he knew her? If so, he didn't remember, but that was normal.

She eyed him as she walked through the swinging doors to the kitchen. She couldn't place him. Oh well. There were a lot of regular customers. He was just one more.

Ho Boy

Madge Darby picked up the phone and said, "Yeah?"

"Don't you ever say, 'Hello,' like normal people?" her sister, Marlene asked, not for the first time.

"No, why should I? I know it's you, and if it's not, then somebody wants something. No one calls me to say, 'Hello.'"

"Uh huh. Well I am calling because something is bugging me."

"You didn't call to say, 'Hello'?"

"No, Madge. I called because I have news for you. Well, I think I do, if I am right about this. Are you sitting down?"

"Yes I am sitting down. You're lucky I wasn't sleeping."

"Madge."

"What?"

"He's here."

"Who's… no."

"Yes. Pretty danged sure."

"Holy Mother."

"I know."

"What's he doing there?"

"Having lunch with some kids. Like he's looking for someone."

"Holy Mother, again."

"What do you want to do?"

"Do? What should I do?"

"Well, he might know me. He looked at me like he remembered something."

"Tell him I've retired and moved away. Get a phone number."

"Madge, do you think…?"

"I think nothing yet. Are you sure it's him? Chiseled nose, blond hair, toothy smile?"

"Oh, it's him, all right. The more I look at him, the more I know it's that Michael Harris, only, you know, older, like the rest of us."

"Well, if he starts asking questions, ask a few of your own, like where he disappeared to. No, don't ask that. He's clueless, as far as I know, so don't stir things up. Just see if you can get some information and call me after work."

"OK, Sis. Gotta go. Sam Jenkins just walked in the door with a bunch of council members trailing their God-awful smoke. Cigars! I'll call later."

Marlene took the order from the smoke-enshrouded politicians before going to check on Michael Harris, him sitting there like a normal person for all the world to see. *Well, wouldn't Big Bart have something to say about this. Hmm, what he doesn't know won't hurt him, I say. Behind bars, especially.*

"How's your lunch? Everything OK here?" she asked the table in general. Mouths full of burgers and whatnot, the answers were muffled. Deke, however, had warmed to his task.

"Do I know you?" he asked, screwing up his courage, reading her name badge, "Marlene? You look familiar. Have you worked here long?"

"No, just practically my whole life. You look like someone I knew once. Name of Michael."

Deke/Michael nodded. "I worked here. A long time ago."

"Yes, yes, I remember now." Sly Marlene, she wasn't giving away the farm. Not yet. Oh no. There was too much at stake here.

They chitchatted for a minute. Marlene knew he was working something out in his slow as molasses mind, she could see that hadn't changed.

"May I ask you something, Marlene?" Without waiting for an answer, he said, "Madge was good to me, and I think I owe her something. Is she still around? It *was* Madge, right?"

Good to you? "Yes, Madge, Madge. She's, uhm, she's retired and living… in the hills." Which was not entirely false. "What do you want?"

"I don't want anything. I'd like to talk to her, if I could. That's all."

"Well, we don't give out phone numbers here, but give me yours and I'll see what I can do. She, ugh, she's not around too much these days." She wanted to add, *thanks to you*, but he wouldn't understand. And Big Bart wouldn't, either.

Deke and his posse of teenagers left Keebler's disappointed. Stevie especially wanted something momentous to happen, an epiphany for Deke and his big box of puzzle pieces known as his PAST. And she wanted to be there to witness it!

Their drive home was naptime quiet. The girls daydreamed, Farley drove along with the taste on his tongue of good French fries and the kick of pink bean soup. And, in Deke's brain, there was a stir of the molasses. Just a stir. It made him cock his head and listen for something.

Deke wasn't back in Felix and Juana's house ten minutes before the phone rang. The girls and Farley left him at the gate, and he planned to take a little nap while they were getting Henry's precious red convertible Isabel the Edsel back to Salinas with nary a scrape nor mishap.

That whole business this morning tired Deke out. He flopped down on the bed to rest and the phone right next to his head rattled and jangled a bell in his tender ear.

"Hello?" he rasped, unused to the phone.

"This Michael?" said a hard female voice.

"Uhm, Michael, yes. Who's this?"

"Well, it's Madge, you must have been expecting me. I guess you'll want to talk."

Confused, Deke said, "I, ugh, yes, sure, yes, Madge, thanks for calling! I'd love to talk to you."

"Well, you'll have to meet me here at the ranch."

"I see. What ranch is that?"

"Seriously? You don't remember?"

"No Ma'am. I remember you, a little. And I remember Keebler's, and my job, and bread. I remember washing mountains of dishes and I remember how to make tomato soup. But, I don't remember any ranch."

"What do you want from me then, if you don't remember?"

"I… want to pay you for a loaf of bread."

"Come again?"

"I said, I…"

"I heard you. What in the world do you want to pay me for a loaf of bread for? What in God's name are you talking about?"

"It's a long story, Madge, but if you'll let me tell it…"

"Never mind. You can tell me when you get here. Do me a favor, act like you're applying for a job. And come alone. Don't bring any of that gaggle of kids with you."

"The kids were my ride to Keebler's today. I don't drive."

"Well, take the bus. Get off at Broadway. I'll have someone pick you up and bring you to the Hills. Come for lunch tomorrow. And don't be late. It seems we have a lot to discuss."

All Deke had to discuss was the $100 bill in his pocket, symbol of his appreciation. But, whatever. He'd go to lunch at the Ranch, wherever that was. He knew how to take a bus to King City.

Another Excursion

Deke's assurance of his safety did nothing to satisfy Tate's worrying nature. He was going where? On a bus to an unknown ranch somewhere in South County, picked up by who knows who? Was he kidding?

No, and here she was, taking him to the bus station in Monterey in her mother's pick up.

"I'll be fine, Tatie. I am just going to see Madge and give her this $100 bill burning a hole in my wallet and be free of that... responsibility. She's on some ranch that I am supposed to remember, so that will be a good thing, to go there, right? Madge was... is a nice lady. Just sharp on the edges, you know? A hard life, being a baker and waitress forever."

"But by yourself on a bus? I don't like it. Rebecca would not be happy. Promise me you'll call or be on that 5pm return bus, because I will be here waiting for you. Don't be late."

He'd heard that somewhere before. Deke kissed his daughter on the forehead and said, "Yes, Ma'am!" flashing her that painfully beautiful smile, teeth and all.

A bus to King City was no big deal and Deke arrived at Broadway without issue, unless you include right off the bat giving his tuna sandwich snack to a homeless man. He wouldn't reveal that little fact to Tate, who made him the sandwich and thought he was too generous with the homeless. But, he felt related to them, a cousin, obliged to wrap his arms around them, in a figurative way. The least he could do was offer food.

A muscular, dark skinned man with a big round head and beautiful pearlescent grin picked him up in a green '49 Ford truck with Hills Ranch written in green and gold script on the door. *Ohhh, Hills… Ranch. OK. But I still don't remember it.*

"Mr. Michael?" said the behemoth. "Ready to go?"

Deke nodded and got in the truck. He grasped at a name, which popped into his head in yellow, like on a marquee: *Big Tandy, Strongest Man in South County.*

"Wait a minute. I know you." The giant smiled to hear it. "You are Big Tandy. You are… Madge's friend? I don't remember."

"I work for Miss Madge. And she's my friend. She keeps us all in the carnival shows, traveling around the western states, *performing the extra-ordinary for the ordinary*. Off the road, off-season, that is, I do whatever Miss Madge wants. Right now, she wants me to bring you to her, Mr. Michael."

Deke said, "Call me Deke. It's what I go by."

"You aren't Michael Harris?"

"Yes, my full name is Michael Harris Harley, but I'm called Deke. It's a long story."

"Tell me. We have a ways to go."

Back in the day, Deke/Michael had kept himself to himself, but they all knew there was a story lurking in there. Big Tandy wanted to know. Deke filled the 40-minute bumpity-bump truck ride with everything he could think of. He usually didn't like telling the story, but Big Tandy inspired one to talk and Big Tandy took it all in. By the time the two men got to Hills Ranch and Big Tandy jumped out to open the gate, drive through and close it again ("No, no," he said to Deke. "Right now you are a guest. Guests don't open the gate.") Big Tandy knew all about Deke's life on the road, his journey.

Big Tandy knew more about Deke than Deke did, but he kept his mouth closed. No point in scaring the man to death. Leave that to Miss Madge.

The Hills

Madge Darby sat nobly enthroned in a room full of bookshelves, with four tall paned windows shedding soft light in patches across the floor. The shelves overflowed with books. On the big sprawling desk a book lay open in front of Madge, whose regal posture was nothing Deke remembered.

Where was the bedraggled, perspiring baker? The apron? The smell of bread?

"You surprised to see me here?"

"Yes. Yes I am. Aren't you... weren't you a baker? At Keebler's?"

"Oh, I was at Keebler's, all right. It's my sister's place now. I was... well. How can I ever say this to you? I was in a bit of a pickle. It was a safe place to be in the middle of the night. And I know how to bake a loaf of bread. Shall I ring for lunch?"

"Pardon?"

"Would you like to have lunch with me, Michael, in our dining room or here in the library. I usually eat in here, with my books."

Deke stared at Madge as if she had just suggested they have dinner at the Taj Mahal with a flock of peacocks.

This was not what he expected at all.

Lunch was served on a small table in front of the window overlooking a shady garden. The "houseman," Little Joe Trailer (like Big Tandy, on the inside track of Madge's world) took one look at Deke/Michael and skedaddled out of the room. He thought Miss Madge was crazy to let him in this house, but it wasn't his business to make up Miss Madge's mind. It was his business to clean up after her, which made him cautious.

After lunch, Madge got to the point.

So, tell me, Michael…"

"Call me Deke," he said. "Everyone does."

"All right, Deke, if that is your name. Do you want to tell me what happened to you? I've got all day."

Here we go again, thought Deke. He knew he owed her an explanation, and was prepared to do that. But the telling got old, particularly when he was vulnerable, like now, though he couldn't say why. That naked feeling cropped up when a memory floated nearby, waiting to be grabbed by his conscious mind.

Did she mean, what happened to him before he met her? Or, what happened when he left King City? Well, first he'd tell her about IT and then, once that was cleared up, she would know he wasn't operating on all cylinders when he walked away with her loaf of bread, and, for that matter, when he walked into her life in the first place. Then he could tell her the rest of his story.

Madge watched the beautiful face she remembered so well as Deke filled her in on the reality of Deke/Michael Harris Harley. Hard to take, his not remembering her. She knew there was something wrong with him… the headaches, the slow speech, she tried to get him to a doctor, but he wouldn't hear of it. He said, "It's just a headache," but she knew better.

Didn't he remember the rest? What was she going to tell him? Should she tell him anything? What good would it do?

Probably no good at all and would just make him nervous. He looked nervous. This is probably a mistake.

"Madge?"

"Sorry. What?"

"I said, I am sorry about taking the bread. I've brought this $100 as a kind of apology or thank you or an amend, I guess. But, you might see by my story that I was not too "together" at the time, in fact, for whatever time I was here with you in King City. Can you tell me about that? How long was I here?"

Madge took her pulse. Her heart pounded and a thin line of sweat began to appear along her hairline, underneath her curls. She heard every word of his story while her mind thrashed with worry over her own truth, about to come to the light. She couldn't take her eyes off that face, that beautiful face, the face of Michael, her lover.

The soul of patience, Deke/Michael just looked out the window, waiting for Madge to speak. She was taking her good old time, but he didn't mind. Yes, sometimes he was nervous, but Deke had years of practice in the sitting and waiting department. This beautiful window displayed a vista full of entertainments: birds in feeders and baths, sunlight through the oaks, a cow in the distance, two men walking toward the house. Oh, a man and a boy. The man was Big Tandy.

The boy was the spitting image of the young Deke Harley.

"My husband thinks the boy is his, Michael. Deke," Madge whispered from her chair at his side.

And then he remembered. Her. The apartment. The ranch she said was her "family's." The nights with her, tangled up in the sheets, mixing her up with a redheaded girl who called to him in the night.

There were lots of drinks, which conked him out, and they smoked some pot, which made him happy and helped his headaches, but he forgot everything that happened. Like knockout drops.

Oh my God.

"Don't have much of a memory at the best of times, do you?"

Daniel

Deke reached into his pocket, took the little piece of paper with the Adobe House phone number on it and dialed. Jock answered. Deke looked out the window at the threesome talking in the shade of an oak: Madge, Big Tandy and the boy named Daniel.

Deke's hands shook and his eyebrows were dripping sweat onto his eyelids. He tried to make sense with Jock: all he had to do was explain that he would be on a later bus, there were things to learn here, which was true enough, but his words were garbled and his heart oddly heavy and sweetly full at the same time. When he hung up the phone he sat down at the table and couldn't take his eyes away from the boy.

Daniel. His son, Daniel, but not his son. Another not situation.

Deke couldn't take much more, but he had to stay long enough to hear Madge's story. She owed him a story.

Big Tandy and Daniel went off to the Barn and Madge came back up the porch steps to the library door and came in.

She and Deke locked in a staring contest, like, whoever looks away first has to buy the other a drink. Madge's eyes expressed a bag of history, Deke's a state of wonder. The seconds ticked away on the Grandfather clock: tick, tick, tick, tick, while they studied each other's eyes.

Madge lost, of course, by looking away, first at the back of her boy moving toward his horse, then out the window at nothing. At everything. She poured them both a shot of tequila. Deke, not much of a drinker anymore, tossed it back.

"My husband is Big Bart Buchanan. You'll never have heard of him, but around here, and in Southern California, he's got connections. He'll tell you he's in real estate, but I'll tell you right now, he's always got a scheme going and a scam brewing.

"But, he'll never tell you anything, because you will never meet him. He is in jail for life without parole for killing a man. He's been in jail since a few months before you wandered to the back door of Keebler's.

"Yeah, I was working at Keebler's. I hated being alone up here in the night at first when the boys were working and Big Bart was gone for good. My boys, Big Tandy and them. When they work the circuit with the sideshows and fairs, they're away for weeks. So, I had my little apartment down in town and set my mind to some honest work at the old family place to fill the time.

"You came along and I was lonely. I couldn't figure you out, though. You were handsome and all, but different. I thought you were hiding something, but, hell, aren't we all? So, I let down my hair and had some fun with you. I liked you. But you never took it to heart. It was like you weren't really there, really "in it" with me. You were off somewhere fighting your own demons, and I imagined yours were at least as scary as mine. Hell, my demons had fiery breath and swishing tails and the females were layin' eggs.

"Anyway, I wasn't really surprised when you left. I am older than you and I felt you had another agenda and were just biding your time until your headache was gone.

"I was surprised, however, by the present you left in my womb. Now that scared the bahooties out of me, because Bart would find you and have you shot down in the street if he knew." Deke's eyes flew open in surprise.

"Sorry. Bart will never find out. As I said, he thinks Daniel is his. I arranged for a couple of conjugal visits at Folsom, and Big Tandy and Little Joe are my men. They will never let me down. They and my sister are the only ones who know."

"Marlene," said Deke.

"Yes, Marlene. And now you. I probably should have left you out of it, but I have a strange streak of honesty in me, and I thought you should know. And anyway, after you left, Marlene showed me an article about your disappearance from the Rodeo Grounds, but by then I knew I was pregnant, and I couldn't afford to get involved. I'd taken enough risks as it was, considering the situation. And you were gone, so what help would I be?"

"How long?"

""What?"

"How long was I here?" Deke asked. "How long did I stay with you?"

"Six weeks. We spent three of those weeks right here, at the ranch. We had a lovely time, but I suppose you don't remember.

"We had just gone back into town when you vanished. It spooked Marlene, who was in the kitchen at Keebler's. One minute you were there, drinking coffee, the next minute you were gone. 'Into thin air,' she said. She never mentioned a missing loaf of bread."

December 1963

Big Sur
The Underside of Bixby Bridge

It all started with a phone call: Stevie and Farley, each in their own bed in their own homes and on their usual phones.

Stevie patted them on their backs for the success of the big King City Expedition. As to the true outcome of Deke's little luncheon at Madge's Hills Ranch, it would excite her greatly if she knew, no doubt.

Stevie's idea of the success was simple: Deke and Madge got together, he gave her the folded up $100 bill, and Madge told him he'd been around Keebler's for about six weeks.

Stevie said to Farley that night on the phone, "Deke had a funny look on his face, but I can imagine he would! Another six weeks lost! All he remembers are dishes, cigarettes, the headaches and one soup recipe, and that's because it was on a piece of paper in his pants pocket."

"Must be hard to be him these days," said Farley, muffled by his covers.

"Yeah, people know things about him that he doesn't. When I asked him about Madge he just said, 'She had a lot to tell me.'"

"You sound normal, Steve. Are you over the *Adam* episode?"

"Oh. No. I can't get too close to Deke, because the smell of him reminds me of *Adam* and the 24 hours he courted me in my head and I get all wobbly-kneed. I don't mean to. I don't want to. And then I get embarrassed because I think he knows. But there it is."

"It'll get better."

"Well, it has to, doesn't it? Tate already thinks I'm depressed about something and not telling her, and she's only half right. I am not telling her. Ever."

"How about Jolene?"

"What about her?"

"Does she think you're acting weird?"

"Hmmm, no. She's preoccupied. She wants to go to Bixby Bridge."

"Wow. To see the site?"

"Yeah, well, I guess not to see the sights, you know? I think she wants to make peace with the bridge, to see where it happened. Too bad she can't get down to the beach."

"I can get her down to the beach."

"What? How?"

"I have the combination to the gate at Bixby Canyon."

"I don't believe this. How do you happen to have that?"

"My dad's law firm represents one of the residents. We've had the combo and a key to his cabin for years. We can go any time. I just have to let him know. He's hardly ever there. Says it's too bohemian for him these days."

"Ha! Ferlinghetti and Kerouac. Well, we won't bother them! We'll be on a mission. Besides, I think I am too young to understand a single word they say. Oh, this is exciting. What time is it?"

"10:30. Don't tell Jo now. Wait till I can call Professor Esta in the morning. When do you want to go?"

The same gaggle of teenagers, sans the 40-year-old Deke, who'd gone quiet since his solo trip to King City, piled four to the seat (one large driver and three relatively small teenaged girls) in the illustrious orange Phoebe for a ride down the coast to Bixby Bridge. Jolene said, "I thank you all for coming with me, but may I go to the bridge alone?" Everyone agreed she should do this however she sees it, they were along for support.

"I'm not keen on your going onto the bridge itself, though," said Farley. "It's dangerous, and the cops don't like it either. Best stay to the side and not too close to the edge."

Jolene jumped out of the truck and went as close to the edge of the cliff as possible without giving Farley a conniption. She could see the beach. The tide was out and it left flat rocks and debris and rivulets of water in its wake. She looked down there for a long time. 14 minutes. Stevie timed it. No one was in a rush. Stevie's just like that.

The support team in Phoebe's cab whispered and plotted their next move while Jolene considered the 280 foot drop, the side of the bridge, the water, the sand, her father, her father's death, the demise of his dreams, the end of the Super Conductor.

Jolene stood still, palms up, almost as if she were holding something out to the sky: an offering. Her eyes gazed upward to a vision only she could see. She looked like the yogini she would become in later years, but now all she thought about was releasing her anxieties and secrets to the wind. Could the wind take them away? Would the ocean wash her clean? Would her father forgive her for letting him leave, letting him die?

Nothing happened, and Jolene was disappointed. She thought she would rid herself of this cursed box of secrets today, but she still felt it clinging to her, sticky.

She thought, *I'll go into the water.*

Farley unlocked the gate to the Bixby Canyon residences, drove through, re-locked the gate behind him, got back into the now dust-covered Phoebe and took the first dirt driveway down into the woods.

The green wonderland was exotic after the dusty ride down the Old Coast Road and into the canyon. The Hosta leaves were huge and fifteen-foot Japonica bushes loomed overhead, creating a lush canopy over the driveway. Redwoods and willows, Madrone and pine, knee deep foliage, vines and weeds and wild mustard, every hue and shade of green, changing shadows, thick vegetation, falling leaves and wild flowers. All sound was hushed, and it made one want to whisper.

Farley stopped at the tiny cabin and parked Phoebe in the shade of an ancient oak. The red door of the cabin was shiny with new paint, but other than that, just a little box in the woods with a roof and a chimney.

They got out of the truck, stretched their legs and were directed by Farley around to the back of the cabin to the outhouse to relieve their bladders. The trail was narrow, feathery leaves brushed their legs. They checked for poison oak.

When all ablutions were performed, Jolene and her followers moved off to the narrow dirt path through this enchanted forest toward the beach. They passed other ghostly quiet cabins, whispered over little footbridges, held onto strategically grown vines, climbed over moss-covered rocks. A jack rabbit paused in its dash to watch them. A few disturbed bees buzzed through Bixby Canyon. Sun filtered through the trees and butterflies flitted in the light.

Enchantments are available everywhere (Fáno says, "We don't do magic. Magic does us."), and this moment, in this little forest, with these earnest, path-following teenagers, whose every step is life-affirming, had an air of tranquility and expectation. A green blanket made of nature's velvet gently covered them, a glowing light led them forward to their destination. Green, green upon green, shadows and green and light and more and more green, every possible green until they came to the beach, and it opened to them like a Sunday morning call to prayer.

There is the beach, Jo thought. *There is the beach where my father died. I will stand on the spot where he died, and I will put him to rest, I will lay this burden down and I will be at peace. And I will be at peace.*

The posse watched as Jolene headed toward the water lapping gently on the sand. She took off her sneakers and socks, set them on a rock and rolled up her jeans as far as they would go. The water tickled her toes. It was Central Coast cold, and her skin shivered.

She walked into the water up to her bare shins. Jolene imagined the box into her outstretched hands, palms up again. This time it appeared, just as she had made it. Its coverings were as good as chains: that box would never open to anyone without the proper spell breaker. Which meant no one would ever open it, since there was not even an imaginary release to this imaginary felted spell. No key. This was a forever situation.

She felt her father's presence, and she hoped that he approved of her symbolic gesture. She didn't want the humming to stop, but she wouldn't mind a new tune.

No flash of lightning, no thunderous voice from the gods' realm, no fireworks. Poof. Just like that. And the box was gone. She tried to imagine it back, since she didn't believe it. But it was gone. In her hands, palms turned up, was an owl feather.

Jolene looked around for her friends, who were sitting atop a big boulder waving to her.

Jolene felt oddly complete and expectant at the same time. She felt a weight off her chest, like someone who had been sitting on her for three years suddenly decided to get up and let her breathe.

Old Joe

The line of teenagers, led by Jolene, quietly headed back to the enchanted forest from the beach. They stood underneath the Bixby Bridge and looked up into the network of its construction, a monumental structure, beautiful, fierce and strong. So different from the Schulte Road Bridge, itself a hobbit compared to this giant.

They approached the trailhead but turned as a group to give a final salute to Chuck and the beach under Bixby Bridge, the place he chose (or chose him) for departing this earth.

When they turned around, a small and extremely wrinkled old man stood on the path. In his tiny left hand he held a miniature cane. In his right hand he carried a .22 caliber rifle, not miniature.

Around his neck hung a big slate on a piece of butcher's twine.

Jolene and the old man inspected each other. She said, "I know who you are. You are a caretaker here. I don't remember your name, but you found my father. When he crashed his car on the beach. You... don't speak."

The ancient one nodded and pointed to her.

"I am Jolene Huffington."

He took a piece of chalk out of his pocket and wrote on the slate. "You are Jo Huff."

"No, I'm..."

He shook his head. "Your art name. New name. Jo Huff," he wrote.

Jolene looked confused. The old man's eyes twinkled. "You'll see. It's written in your future. Come." He put the chalk back in his pocket and turned to go.

"All of us?" Jo asked, a little afraid to follow him alone, but she was curious.

He stopped to regard Jolene's friends. He took the chalk out again and wrote, "I am Timmons. Old Joe, to you. Come. All of you."

He took them on a circuitous route to his cabin, forging a trail through the underbrush which closed behind Farley, last in line, who turned to review the path they'd taken and found only perfect, un-trodden knee-deep green foliage.

They stopped at a clearing with a small cabin. On perches by the door were three untethered owls, one of which winked at Jolene, who looked down at the feather in her hand.

The cabin was reminiscent of Fáno's work: a thick thatched roof, full of birds' nests, extended far out over the hodge-podge walls, affording shade in an otherwise sunny spot. Old Joe set down his .22 by the door and turned to face his guests. He wrote on his slate. "Cold Water. One Minute."

He went into the cabin, took a tin cup off its hook above the tiny counter, got a bottle of water out of the cooler and went back outside. When they all had a drink and admired the taste of the water and petted the owls and let them kiss their necks with their owlish beaks, the welcome ritual was complete. Old Joe invited Jolene inside.

"It's good," he wrote for all to see. "Don't worry about this old man." He grinned and opened the door.

Jolene, twirling the owl feather in her hand, surveyed the room: feathers and rocks, stump stools and table, handmade clay dishes, sink in the corner, wood stove, stack of wood, sleeping pallet by the stove.

She couldn't help saying, "Stevie would love this," to which Old Joe wrote, "Sometime, yes. Today, you."

"OK," she said. He gestured to one of the petrified stumps. They sat in silence for a moment. Then Old Joe wrote, "I knew you'd come. Sooner or later. If it was my father, I would come." She nodded.

Jolene asked, "Did my dad explode?"

Old Joe cocked his head, as if to say, 'What a question!" Then he slowly shook his head side to side.

He erased the other words with his chalk-covered sleeve and wrote, "No one asked about this, so I saved it 4 U. I knew you'd come."

He got up, agile for someone 200 years old (it seemed to Jolene) and went to the wood stove, to the mantel above, obviously his altar. He took down an object wrapped in black velvet and handed it to Jolene, who knew what it was the minute it was in her hand. She unwrapped the  velvet to find the Super Conductor's Magic Wand.

Jolene's Magic Wand

Jolene lay on her small bed in the Art Box, staring at the half sun/half moon and stars above her. She twiddled the Magic Wand in her hands. She didn't believe in magic, but enough weird things were happening to make her begin to believe in something. Otherwise, how did Old Joe appear from Nowhere?

And the wand - the conductor's baton. Chuck left it to her in his will. At least, if he wrote a will, she knew it was in there. He said, in an expansive mood, that when he died he would leave her all his musical instruments, his sheet music and the baton, which were the only things he cherished besides her.

No one ever found the will, or the baton, and thought them both lost to the surf.

She held the baton in her two hands. It was beautiful, made in the 19th century, thicker than modern batons, ebony, with a slim carved ivory cap on one end, around which his conducting fingers fit perfectly. She played with the ivory cap, imagining his fingers, his music, his flights of fancy, his moments of madness.

When she thought of her father, Jolene tried to remember the good things, and not the burdens and secrets. She focused on the happier times, the music and the playful spirit, before his demons got the better of him. Perhaps now she could let go of the resentment and embrace her own life.

The ivory cap twisted in Jolene's hand, and at first she thought it was loose. On closer inspection, she saw that it was screwed on. *Cool,* she thought. *If it screws on, then it screws off.* She laughed. Probably a tiny flask.

She unscrewed it and carefully tipped the baton, or Magic Wand if you will indulge her for one more moment, toward her other hand and out spilled 25 perfect, rather large diamonds with a tiny piece of rolled up paper on which was written in Chuck's handwriting:

"For Jo Huff's college fund. I did not steal her future."

The new Jo Huff would one day say, "Knock me over with an owl feather."

Excerpt from Stevie's 1960s
Honors English Journal
Christmas Vacation Entry 1963
Deke Interrupted

I can write about Deke Harley's return to the farm now because the police and the press know, and "case solved," or almost, although still no clue as to the whackers.

But, it makes for a good story: there will be an article in the Acorn and Deke will be the famous and mysterious returned Cowboy.

I'd wager he's never rounded up a cow in his life. Must be the boots. We're glad he's not referred to as the Drifter, so named by the press at the time of the mysterious 1950 disappearance.

His return brings us to the end of a thirteen-year story and the beginning of a new one. He's not keen on being a famous anything and keeps a low profile.

He has changed I hear, although I was only one and a half at the time of his disappearance. The one photo in existence of the old Deke shows him lean and intense, smoke from his cigarette curling up around his head.

Now, after years of recovery from a major and perfectly placed whack upon the head, he is a softer version: handsome, kind of sweet, wise in a slow way.

Deke's last thirteen years have been no picnic in the park. He has endured three or four surgeries, a loss of long-term memory

– mostly his whole life before the bump on the noggin and some after. He regained some memory after the last surgery, which followed a fall off a ladder.

He writes everything down in order to practice remembering it. His notebook has lines written in it like, "constellations, big dipper, full moon, harvest moon, moon pie, high noon."

Or, "Fox, mail box, yellow dress, red shoes. 1946. She said, 'Like magnets.'"

Or, "mailman, delivered at noon, Frank, philosopher, looked like Walt Whitman, Long white hair, full white beard. 1948?"

I had asked, "What do you write, Uncle Deke?"

He handed me his book, a thick spiral-bound pad with lined paper. He smiled and said, "Just between us writers."

His writing is small and loose with loopy Ys and Gs. The notes are by someone who lived outside of his mind for ten years and is still trying to get back in.

Deke is now living in the cottage while the Rodriguezes are away. What will happen next in the continuing story of Deke Interrupted?

$100

Deke kept to himself in the cottage for the next few days. Without Fox's ability to hide in plain sight, he fabricated several headaches. Deke had no cocktail party banter in him just now.

He heard about the Bixby Bridge Expedition from Tate and wondered what was next on their agenda, since Stevie had in mind to fix the world. He'd best stay out of her way. He could see that his niece had determination through to her core.

Ha. He knew that from the get-go, when she was *Sam*. He could tell a lot about a person in the first few minutes. Deke thought most people were predictable and true to the bone. How you saw them first, that's how they'd be until the last.

Except for Madge. But, he hadn't "seen" her before, considering he remembered only a fragment of their story, so that blew his theory already. He guessed he saw what he wanted to see, or what he was able to see, and he didn't see the ranch, or remember Big Tandy or Little Joe or a lot of other elements until he was up against them, face to face.

Once he saw them, and Madge nudged his recollection of the warm sheets and breakfast in bed, the flood of memories wouldn't stop. Now he remembered rides over the hills on two ponies, his and hers; steaks on the Weber Charcoal Grill; holding her in his arms and calling for a name he couldn't find.

And the boy! He promised Madge he would not come to the ranch again, but the boy! Knowing his son lived an hour away crushed his heart: he could not, would not ever be Daniel's father.

What irony; after thirteen years of nothing I come back and find two families. Busy little johnson you've got there, Dekie boy. Even when you're half dead.

How could he court Fox without telling her this new secret? Could he keep the knowledge of his son from her, she whom he hoped to wed? Can you make marriage vows with this kind of burden on your soul?

He couldn't tell her. He'd have to carry this one to the grave. What would it serve? He couldn't claim him as his son anyway, so it would only stir the pot.

He chose to say the $100 bill cleared his conscience. He thanked Stevie and the posse for his expedition and did his best to put that episode in King City to rest by placing the knowledge of his precious look-alike son in a box and setting it on a back shelf in the closet. At least, since the box wasn't real, no one would find it.

Ben Lomond
Fox Awakens

Fox awoke every morning at the cabin in Ben Lomond with Deke on her mind, as usual. Only now it was a new theme, a new tune, a mantra, for or against: "yes or no, do I or don't I, will I or won't I?"

By Tuesday morning she had made up her mind. She packed her few belongings and prepared to meet Nana at the bottom of the long driveway.

Fox looked forward to the walk down the hill. It gave her more time to consider her decision. All through the week, in which she spoke to no one, ate when she was hungry, slept when she was tired, read books without retaining one word and spent hours by the pond contemplating and naming the fish (Hank Williams, Peter, Paul and Mary, President Kennedy) she considered options.

By the time she arrived at the row of mailboxes at the bottom of the hill, the end of her sojourn was in sight, there was only the one choice and she knew it and chided herself for pretending there was ever any other way. She was finished thinking about it and she would just have to pick up her boots and move on.

Fox never experienced being alone before. Never. On the very first morning in the cabin, when she awoke with no chores, no demands on her time, no music in her ears from the next room, no questioning or opinionated teenagers to pester her, she felt empty. It wasn't a good empty, like a clean cup, but a sad empty, a lonely empty, a cup with scum in the bottom.

Fox knew if she ever planned to be alone again, she'd have to do it with some purpose in mind. This idling away the hours in the mountains with the blue jays was for the birds. Fox, as she discovered, was no contemplator. She was a doer.

She felt lighter, having come to her decision.

The Hobbit House
Sweet Farm, Carmel Valley
A Cousins' Confab

Stevie, Tate and the newly crowned Jo Huff sat knee to knee in the Hobbit House Middle, inside the big yellow circle.

"Farley told me as long as I don't do it for purposes of fraud, I can call myself Bozo the Clown or Tarzan or Little Miss Muffet, if I want to. I like Jo Huff. It has a nice ring to it."

"What about that old man? What do you make of Old Joe?"

"Well, it wasn't magic, if that's what you're thinking. He lives in the canyon, he heard my dad's crash, he went to the crash site, he found my dad, and he took the baton home with him to save for me. He wanted to make sure I got it. He said he knew I'd come. I guess if I want to show it to anyone other than you, meaning my mum, I'd better just say I found it. Otherwise it gets complicated." She should know.

"And the owl feather?" Stevie was on it.

"She flew over me at the right time."

"I'll say."

"No, really, it was just a coincidence. There is no magic, no meaning in it."

"Then why do you call it a Magic Wand?"

Jo stared at Stevie. Sometimes her cousin could be so annoying. "That's just a story, Steve. It's make believe."

"OK. So it was just a coincidence that your box disappeared and an owl happened along at the perfect time and just happened to drop a feather into your hands, an owl feather, Jo, an owl feather: symbol of wisdom, of good medicine. And then the person who found your dad and kept the baton (and at whose home the owl happens to live) appears on the threshold of the jungle and invites you home and "Ta Da!" That got Jo's attention.

"I can't believe you, Jo. It couldn't be more fantastical if it had been written by one of the Brothers Grimm. And besides, if you'll think about it for just one tiny minute, you'll remember that you created the imaginary box in the first place and made the gesture to throw it somewhere, so you can't tell me you don't believe in some kind of magic. It doesn't matter that we don't know what's in the box," she added, with a hint of a scowl.

"It was just a ritual."

"Uh huh."

"He didn't steal the diamonds, either."

Jo and Stevie looked at Tate, who up to this point had kept quiet. "What?" they asked.

"Old Joe. He knew the diamonds were there. He saw your name, your new name, so he must have seen the diamonds. It's a miracle to me he didn't just take them and make the baton disappear. No one would have ever known if he did."

"That's crazy," Nana said later, when Jo showed the baton to her mother. "Where did you find it?"

"I told you. In the woods under the bridge," which was true.

"So what's such a miracle about that? It flew out of the car, it landed in the bushes, you found it three years later."

"Ah. Well, the mystery continues. Open your hand." She unscrewed the carved ivory top and tipped it into her mother's open hand. Out spilled the diamonds. Jo unrolled the note and gave it to her mother.

Have you ever seen anyone faint? There's this moment, before they fall over, wherein all the blood literally drains out of the top of the body and pools in the legs. The heart rate has increased for whatever reason (heart attack, whack on the head, shocking news, a handful of diamonds from the dead) and the pumping blood, usually so reliable, can't keep up with the beats. The person's face turns white. Sometimes their eyes roll back in their head.

If Nana had been standing up, she would have fallen down. At least she had the presence of mind to close her hand around the diamonds. As she was sitting on the piano bench when she fainted, she merely leaned toward the 88 keys and hit about 50 of them with her left arm. The noise startled her and prevented a full on crash into oblivion.

Jo put her hand on her mother to steady and comfort her. It was a shock. Perhaps her delivery could have been better. But what else could she do? This discovery, magic, miracle, whatever it was, had to be shared with her mother.

Carmel Beach

Fox and Deke

Fox and Deke strolled down the beach in bare feet. They did not hold hands, as they might have done thirteen years earlier, but much had changed: a lot of water under that bridge.

They walked side by side in an awkward unison. The water skipped over their feet and splashed around their ankles. The blue water went on forever, the afternoon sun shone in their eyes and caused them each to squint.

It was New Year's Day, 1964, a time for new beginnings. Although he was grateful for the invitation to walk and talk, Deke worried. He knew this had momentous possibilities but there were several ways it could go.

They got all the way to the kelp piles by Stevie's favorite bench before Fox spoke. She looked out to the bay for something to focus on. She found a surfer and kept her eyes on him. He was sliding all the way into the beach and jumping off his board before she said, "I don't want to marry you, Deke."

"Fox, I..."

"Don't talk. Please. Just listen. You asked me to think about this, and I have, for a whole week, by myself. Just listen to what I have to say."

"All right, Fox. I am all ears."

The surfer climbed back on his board and paddled out to sea. Deke and Fox watched.

Fox dug her heels into the wet cold sand. She gripped the broad beach with her toes, as if that would keep her from flinging off the earth. She began again.

"Deke, I have never wanted marriage, from you or anyone. I don't know why, and I don't care why. There is something in me that says a resounding NO whenever it comes up. And particularly now, in this circumstance, with you appearing out of the sky and everything topsy-turvy.

"But, I will do it for Tate. I know I said the other day that I wouldn't do that, but I have changed my mind. On one condition, and that is that we do it as you say, as friends. No expectations. Day by day.

"There is more, but I can't talk about it yet, because it is not fully formed, but the only way this can happen is to make it about Tate and not as a biggie-wow-wow glorious reunion, because, at least for me, it is not working out that way. I have changed, you have changed.

"But, Tate is growing up, and she deserves to have this. So I will do it for her, quietly, just family. And I don't know about the sleeping arrangements yet, because frankly, the whole idea of it scares the socks off my feet. But, I'll do this if you agree to take it a day at a time."

Deke wanted to reach out to Fox, to touch her, to take her hand in his and kiss it and tell her he loved her and that even when he didn't remember her, he was still loving her and missing that love. He wanted to tell her that the thirteen years were pure hell and that being here with her and Tate and on the farm with the family had made him better already, even before this moment when she agreed to marry him.

He was better because of love, even though she didn't love him. He didn't know how that worked, but he knew it was so. He could live with that.

He turned away from his view of the surfer, still paddling, and took Fox's hand in the least aggressive way he could. He took her hand and held it lightly, and said, "I will be your friend, Fox."

His own hot news was safely tucked in the latest imaginary box on the compound.

Men all do about the same thing when they wake up.
                              - John Steinbeck, *Cannery Row*

JANUARY 1964
Sweet Farm, Carmel Valley
Dekie and Foxie

"Where did they go, do you think?" Deke asked Fox one morning over breakfast in the garden.

Their truce developed without the use of white flags, or any surrender. They both just decided. They came to the party. The party was weird, but they were attending it, and they were the only guests, which was what made it weird.

But they each get an A for effort. It's hard to get acquainted with someone you used to know inside and out. Old habits crop up, old ways of conversation, inside jokes, special words, some of which fall flat on the floor. Fox's face showed the confusion about her feelings, or lack of them, and Deke suppressed his feelings, or the strength of them.

"What? Who?"

"Dekie and Foxie. Where did they go?"

"I suppose that's a rhetorical question?"

"Not really. You'll say I have too much time on my hands and I think too much, but I wonder about who we were. Who we are. Are we new or are we the sum of our years, made up of all the who we weres?"

"Can't you just relax and enjoy my company? You make me nervous when you go all philosophical."

"John Steinbeck says that when two people meet, each one is changed by the other so you've got two new people. So that means we're just different every day and affected by everyone we meet all the dang time. No wonder nothing is stable in this world."

"Deke."

"What?"

"Eat your berries."

Deke laughed. "You'll get used to me," he said. "Maybe you'll like me even better."

Jo Huff and Her Mother

This latest argument, or if you prefer, exchange of heated words, between Jo Huff and her mother, began over the very name, Jo Huff.

"What's wrong with Huffington? It's a perfectly good name," Nana said.

"Nothing is wrong with it, Mum. But, look, here it is, in Dad's handwriting. Isn't it lovely? Please, just look at it. It's kind of permission from a Huffington to make my own way, isn't it? It's just a name, Mum, like a… stage name. An artist's name."

"Your Grand Mama Charlotte won't like it."

"I don't care. It's just a name. It's like taking my name and making art out of it. Give it a rest. Think about something else."

"OK, where do you suppose those diamonds came from? Did he buy them? Steal them? What are we to think of a conductor's baton full of poached diamonds?"

"They're not poached! Daddy wouldn't steal anything."

"Oh no? You don't know your crazy alcoholic father as well as you think you do."

"I know he wouldn't leave me stolen diamonds."

"Well, that remains to be seen."

"What does that mean?"

"It means you'll have to give them to me and we'll see where he got them."

"No."

"What?"

"No. He gave them to me. He left them for me. They are not yours to play with."

"I hardly plan to play with them, Jolene. The idea is to find their source."

"Well, as far as I am concerned, the source was Daddy's Conductor's Baton. My Magic Wand."

"Pish."

"Your attitude amazes me, Mum. All you do is hunt all over the south of England chasing rainbows or sitting in that green chair at Grand Mama Charlotte's, cogitating the many keyholes in the universe you haven't tried to fit the stupid key in."

Jo paused in her tirade, her eyes wide as a tiger's. She turned her head slightly, like a puppy when it hears a high-pitched sound. Her eyes focused on the design in the carpet. "Green chair. Oh my God. The green chair."

She shot out of her mother's room and then turned around in the door. She said to Nana, "Don't go away. I'll be right back," as if Nana would ever leave in the middle of this! And then she dashed across the hall to her room, her hair leaving a streak of red behind her.

It was right where she left it in the bottom drawer of her desk, tucked into her pocket dictionary. It meant nothing at the time of discovery, when was that? Sometime last year, spring break, maybe. But now…

Jo rushed back to her mother's room and flopped down on the bed, bouncing her mother's novel and dithering the whiskers of Mesmer the cat, at her feet.

"Mum. Listen to me. This is weird, but, I found this last year and didn't get it, it meant nothing, but I don't think it's nothing, I think it is something. Something important, but I have no idea why."

"What are you talking about, Jolene. You are not making sense."

"No, really, I am. I just… I don't understand the details, but listen to this. It's called, The Green Chair! Daddy wrote this in…" she turned the piece of paper over and stared at the back. Written in pencil on the back was a tiny inscription, which Jo read aloud to her mother:

> *for Jo*
> *November 1960*

Jo looked up at her mother before she started reading:

> *Behind the green chair*
> *There's a wish and a prayer*
> *There's a song to be sung*
> *And bells to be rung*
>
> *And if you are smart*
> *And open your heart*
> *The news will be good*
> *All over the 'hood*

I'll sing you my songs
All the day long
But you've never heard
Such encouraging words

I'll be there for you
In all that you do
It's incredible, wonderful,
Fabulous news

So take heart my girl
Though I'm in the next world
You're free from now on
Now that I'm gone

The spell is lifted
To you this is gifted
The darkness is over
And you are in clover

Babblety-bee Babblety-boo
I wrote this silly song for you
It means nothing now I know but soon
Bibblety babblety boo

"Well," said Nana. "That's about the silliest thing I ever heard…"

"No, Mum. It's not silly at all. It's a clue."

Fox and Her Sisters

"There is no other choice, you know. Tate is right. I… we owe her this. It's not her fault I'm stubborn and her father is… given to flight.

"And if it makes her happy, I can do it. I've turned something off inside - some running faucet of grief, the drain on my spirit, you know? Up there on Heather's mountain, I put my grief away. I'll do this and see what's next."

"What'll you do about the bed part?" asked Nana.

"I don't know. It may be inevitable, sleeping in the same bed. But I haven't agreed to the rest of it."

"The rest of it used to mean so much to you," Rita said.

"I know. I… just don't get it either, but, it's like he says, we are two new people. We start from some entirely uncharted place. We don't know each other one tiny bit, but we will be husband and wife because we have a child. Does that make us family? Does that automatically put us into life-together-forever-after mode?"

"It's like an arranged marriage," said Rita. "You're expected to fall in love with each other after the wedding. After getting to know each other. Hmmm. Again."

"Yes, well, we'll see about that. And what about your William, Noons," Fox asked. "And the key? Tell us about that."

"You want to discontinue this line of talk about your life?"

"Yes, please."

"OK, well, as to the key thing, listen to this." Nana told her sisters about the magic wand, the diamonds and the poem. She told them all Jolene had told her, which had divine magic enough even without knowledge of the Old Man.

"I can't imagine what those diamonds are worth, or where they came from, and I can't get Jolene to part with them for a minute. So, now I've got a magic wand full of diamonds, a key to nothing and a very crazy poem about a green wingback chair. Oh, and a daughter who wants to be called Jo Huff. I have a feeling that all these voices in my head will stop when this comes together."

"What voices?"

"Oh. I don't know. Perhaps the many voices of Charles Huffington. There's just this constant buzz in my head, like a mob of people trying to talk all at once. And I smell gin sometimes."

"And William?"

"Ah. He's nice about it, because he is a nice man, but I know he finds my key thing a bit tiresome, mostly because my search for a keyhole takes up so much of my time and thoughts. And now all this. He is ready to 'make it real,' as he says. He also says, though, that first I must 'find a new hobby.'

"It just means such an upset - Lady Charlotte, for starters. Even if she likes the match, I mean, it has been three years, and she doesn't have to know about the earlier part, before Charles… before… anyway, she'll not want to see me moving out. I hate leaving her alone, even though I'm not such good company for her, but I can't live with her forever. I can't sneak around. And Jo goes often enough. She loves living at Woolsley and weekends with Grand Mama and holidays in the States at Sweet Farm."

"Are you bringing Will home to meet her?"

"Ha ha, I suppose I'll have to, won't I? Isn't that funny. Taking my lover home to meet my former mother-in-law. Oh, well. Worse things have happened. Maybe she'll like him."

A Wedding

Father Green, the new headmaster at The Day School in Pacific Grove and a Wyman family friend, came to Sweet Farm to perform the long-awaited wedding of the parents of that sweet illegitimate child, Tate Wyman.

Father Green grinned as he walked through the door. His smile reached beyond his red beard and embraced everyone in the room. He gave big hugs all around and, when he came to the bride and groom, standing rigid before him like two plastic decorations lifted from the wedding cake, he laughed and gathered them up in his arms for a three-way bear hug, his specialty with nervous brides and grooms.

Jock and Maria's friends were aghast in the past when Fox and Deke did not marry lickety-split in 1947 upon the surprise news of a baby. And then the rest of it: Deke's sudden disappearance, his possible death, well, who knew what had gone on there - what did she expect with a drifter?

Now they had the chance to make it right!

Fox scoffed at that notion as she packed once again for the cabin in Ben Lomond, this time for her honeymoon. Now that gave her the jitters all the way through.

The morning went smoothly enough: too much emotion for Fox's style, but she resolutely stood her ground on the friendship issue and asked not to have a lot of fuss and overt mushiness about this ceremony.

She whispered to Nana, "This is a practical business, don't they see that?" as Rita came in with bunches of flowers and Tate helped Juana lay brunch on the table and, yes, a cake.

"Don't you see they need this?" hissed Nana, offering a rare insight. "Just think of it as Tate's family ceremony."

"Good idea. That's the truth."

The Episcopal wedding service, established eons ago and handed down through the lineage of inspired Episcopal fathers, didn't leave much room for individual creativity, which suited Fox fine, not interested in writing her own vows. *I do, you do, we all do. Let's just do it*, she thought.

"Love, honor, fine, leave out the 'obey' part, though," Fox said when they discussed the verbiage for the ceremony. "Seems a little silly." The totality of her contribution.

"Aren't you a little hard?" asked her mother in a quiet moment together. "Can you let down your guard, darling girl?"

"Am I not right? It is a little silly."

"It's not that. It is the way you say it. I think you can relax a little. There is no enemy here."

"Deke said the same thing to me. Am I that transparent?"

"Well, I think so, but I am your mother. I think you are afraid. To others, you might just look nervous. Relax now. Nothing bad will come of thees. Only good. You'll see."

Fox and Mama Maria touched brow to brow, in the old way as Maria did with each of her girls when they were young. They stood connected this way, eyes closed, and Fox did relax. She didn't know what was coming next, but she was not afraid.

A Honeymoon

The pond, filled with lilies and pads and darting fish, rippled in the slight breeze. The sun warmed their backs, the bookshelves in the cabin were full of cheap novels and *How Did They Do/Make/Build That?* vacation books - what more could they want?

Perhaps love, but that was not lacking on Deke's part.

Dusk fell and the cicadas spoke. The frogs croaked myriad complaints. The fish stilled and took refuge under rocks.

"Deke-" "Fox-" the two humans said at once.

"Sorry. You go first," Deke said.

"No, you," said Fox, suddenly shy.

Pauses in conversation can be such busy little hallways, with all those thoughts running back and forth. Deke's vocabulary suddenly left him. He was afraid if he opened his mouth he'd be speaking in Tahitian (Nova Scotian, maybe) and she would not understand him.

"I... I wanted to talk about the... I need to discuss the... you said something about the... arrangements. The sleeping arrangements. Not sleeping. I... God, this is hard to say."

Deke rose from the picnic table and walked down to the edge of the pond. He bent down and swished his fingers in the water. So many words stuck in his throat. What was he going to say to her?

He had waited for this moment for three years, since first seeing her in his mind's eye that "waking-up day." He wanted to be with her, touch her red hair, hold her hand, love her, run his fingers along her bony spine, make her sigh, and now, faced with the reality of her, he knew he could not make it so. For so many reasons.

He heard a ribbit and looked to the left where he beheld the ugliest frog he'd ever seen. This 6-pound frog's head outweighed his body, and his pale warts shimmered on a shiny blue-green skin. His ribbit roared like tiny thunder and shook the reeds with its fetid breath. Deke laughed out loud and for some reason, the sound of his own laugh gave him courage. He almost thanked the frog for being so terrifically homely, but the frog was gone.

Deke stood up, walked back to Fox, who sat at the picnic table watching him, and said, "Look, I know you didn't want this and I know I'm not the man you loved so wildly all those years ago. I am not that man. I am a new man. I will be your man if you let me, but I don't expect you'll let me, at least for now. I don't want anything from you, Fox, except to be friends, and to be in Tate's life, and your life, what you'll give me.

"What I am trying to say is, I won't be chasing you. Sex is not my first priority, love is."

Fox couldn't imagine the old Deke, the Deke that was so rudely interrupted mid-life, saying anything close to this. She would wait forever if she expected to see the arrogant, sexy, high-strung Deke emerge. That was then.

Now, she had a nice big wounded bird on her hands. Almost too nice. She missed the tension.

She liked his smile, though, when he offered it. She saw him, when he smiled, saw the old Deke living inside the new. And she had to admit, there was a comforting elegance to his slow speech, and a sweetness to his words.

She nodded. What would she say? *Sure hon, I knew that...?* No. There was no answer, so she nodded again and let it go. Fox had not surrendered her heart to this union, and she didn't know if she would.

They sat in companionable silence as the sky darkened and the woods began its nighttime rustle. The frogs and cicadas made their music, tubas and flutes and strings couldn't compete. Every now and then the frogs and cicadas and their chirpy friends would go quiet, waiting for a big cat to walk through on its path, or a skunk, or raccoon.

Deke said, "What did you want to say, hon?"

Fox took her eyes off the tree squirrel she was watching and looked at Deke. Not for the first time that day, her wedding day, she thought, *What am I doing here? This can't be real.*

She looked at Deke. "You said the other day that you thought you would look for a job."

"Yeah, I think it might be time for that."

"And you no longer look like you're going to die in the next few weeks. Have you fallen down lately?"

"No. Tenderly said, by the way."

She ignored the remark and said, "You could do my job."

"What?"

"You could definitely do my job. It hasn't changed that much."

"You, who Stevie calls the General of Sweet Farm, would give up control for me?"

"Not for you. For me."

"What would you do?"

"Any number of things."

"Want to talk about these things?"

"Yes. How much time have you got?"

"All the time in the world, darlin'... all the time in the world..."

End of

Deke Interrupted

***The Lavandula Series* continues
in Book Three:**

Humming in Spanish

Drawings by the author:

Bird's Eye View of Sweet Farm

Barn Front Elevation

Chapel House Front Elevation

Barn Interior

Chapel House Interior

Adobe House Front Elevation

Adobe House Interior

Sweet Farm Bird's Eye View

SCHULTE ROAD

TO THE VILLAGE

CARMEL VALLEY ROAD

BARN

COTTAGE

ADOBE HOUSE

FRUIT STAND

HOBBIT HOUSE

CHAPEL HOUSE

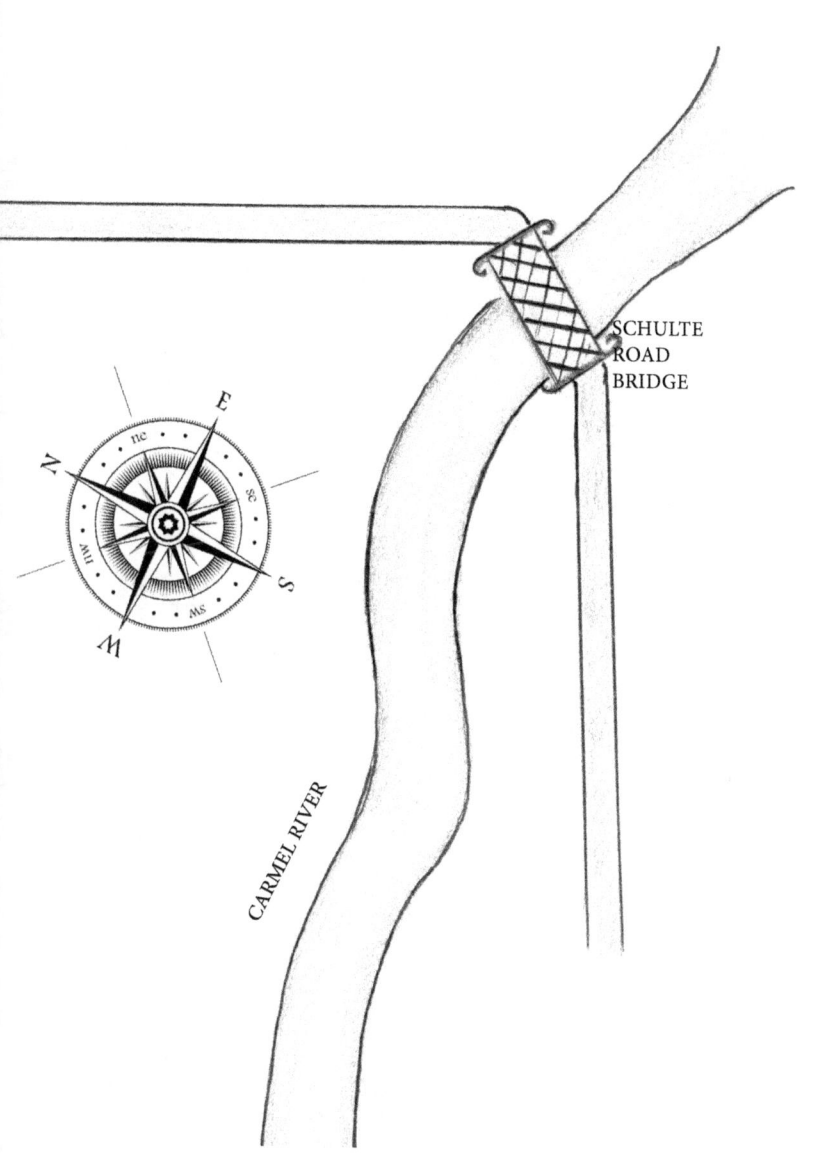

N
E
ne
se
S
sw
W
nw

SCHULTE
ROAD
BRIDGE

CARMEL RIVER

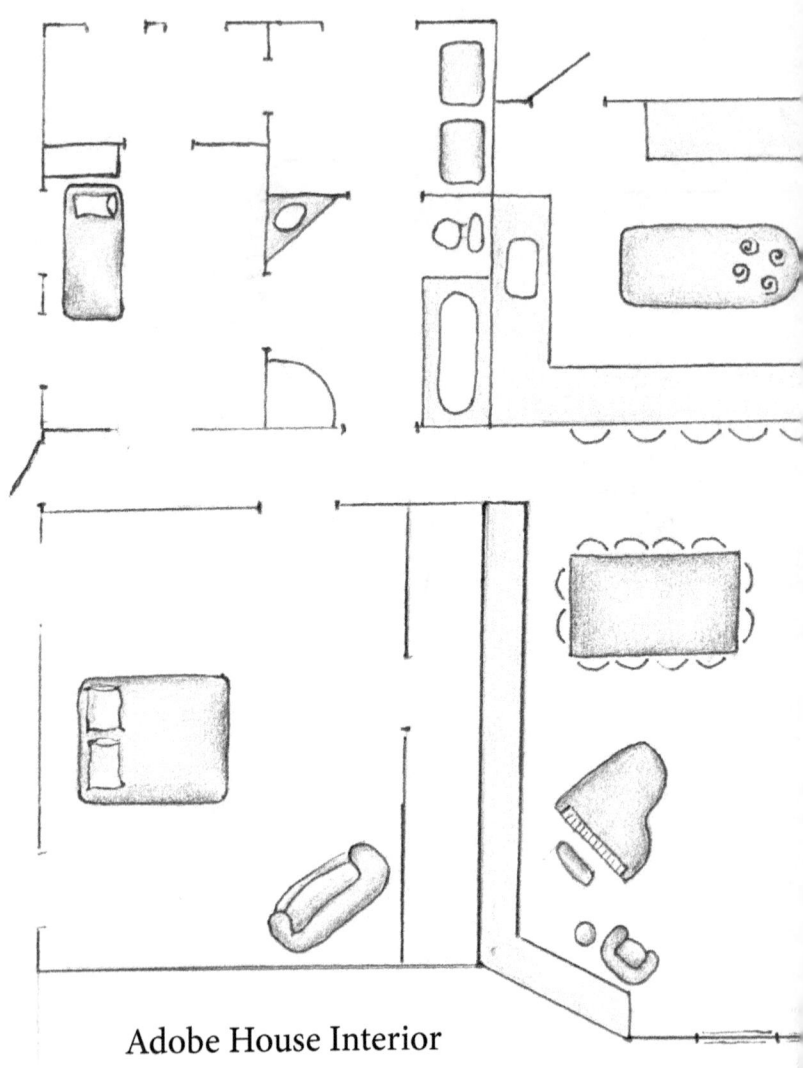

Adobe House Interior

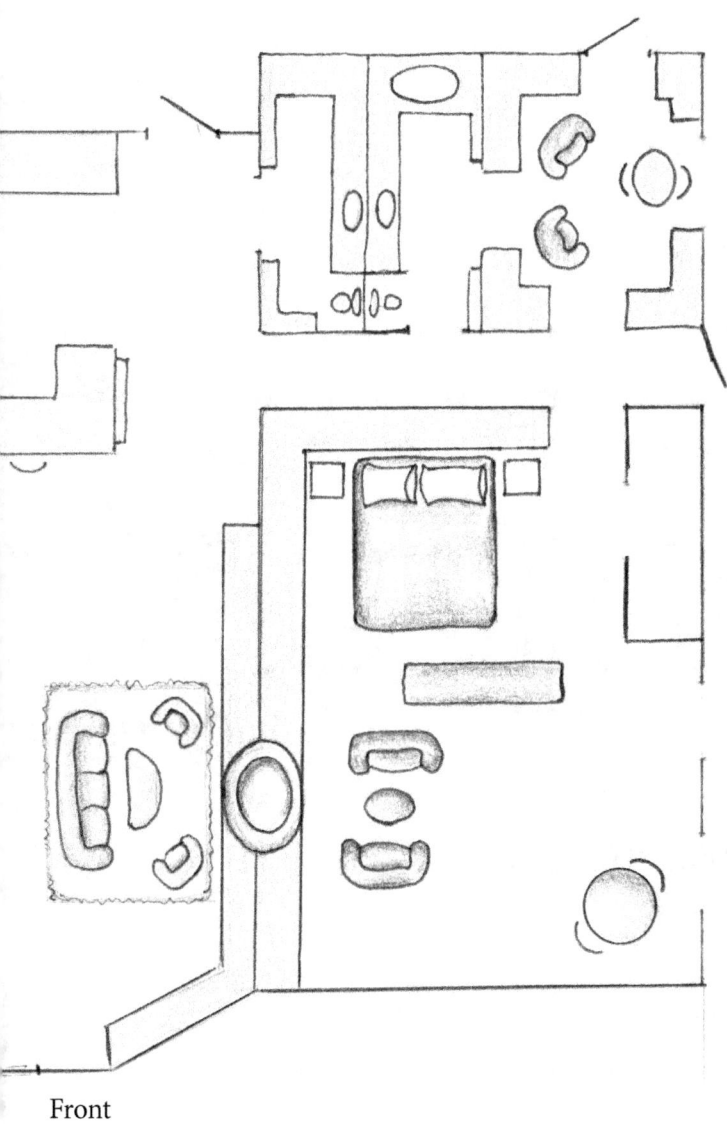

Front

Adobe House Front Elevation

Barn Front Elevation

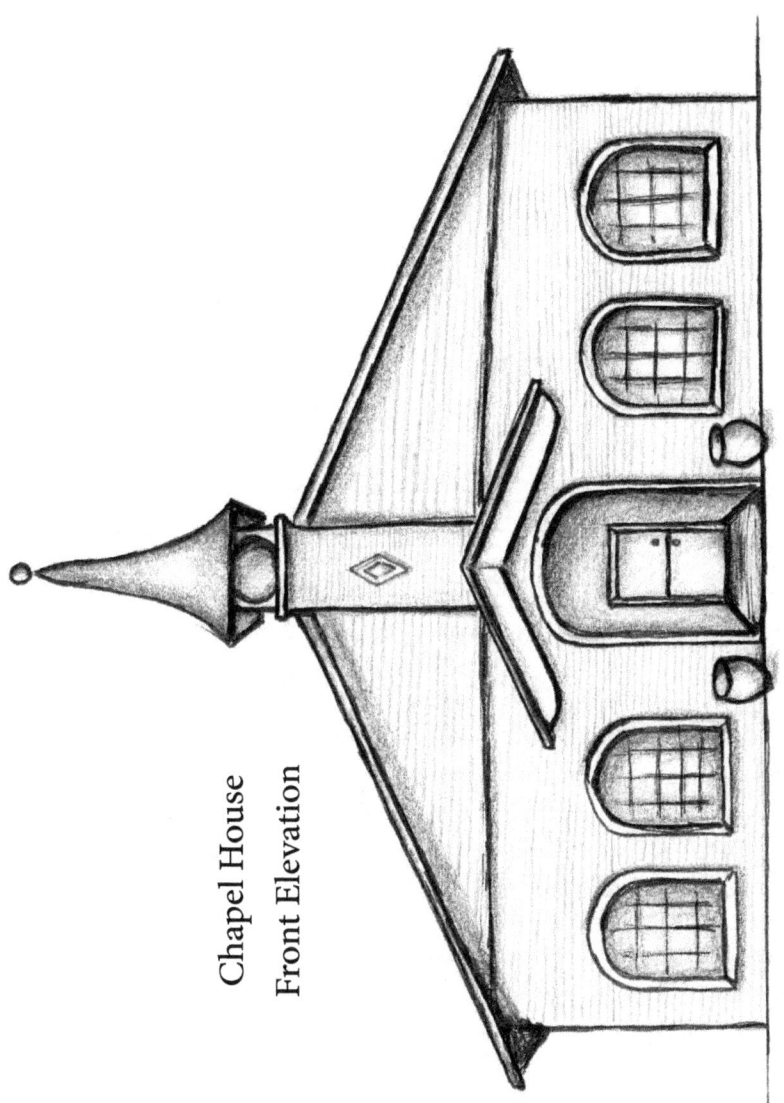

Chapel House
Front Elevation

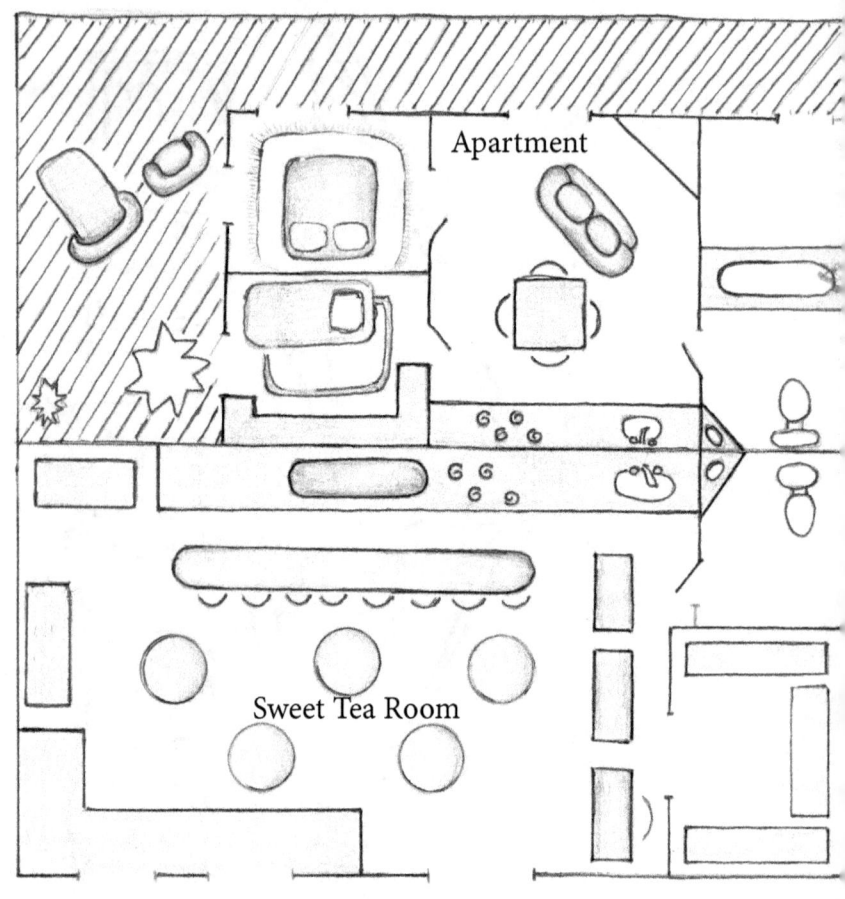

Apartment

Sweet Tea Room

Barn Interior

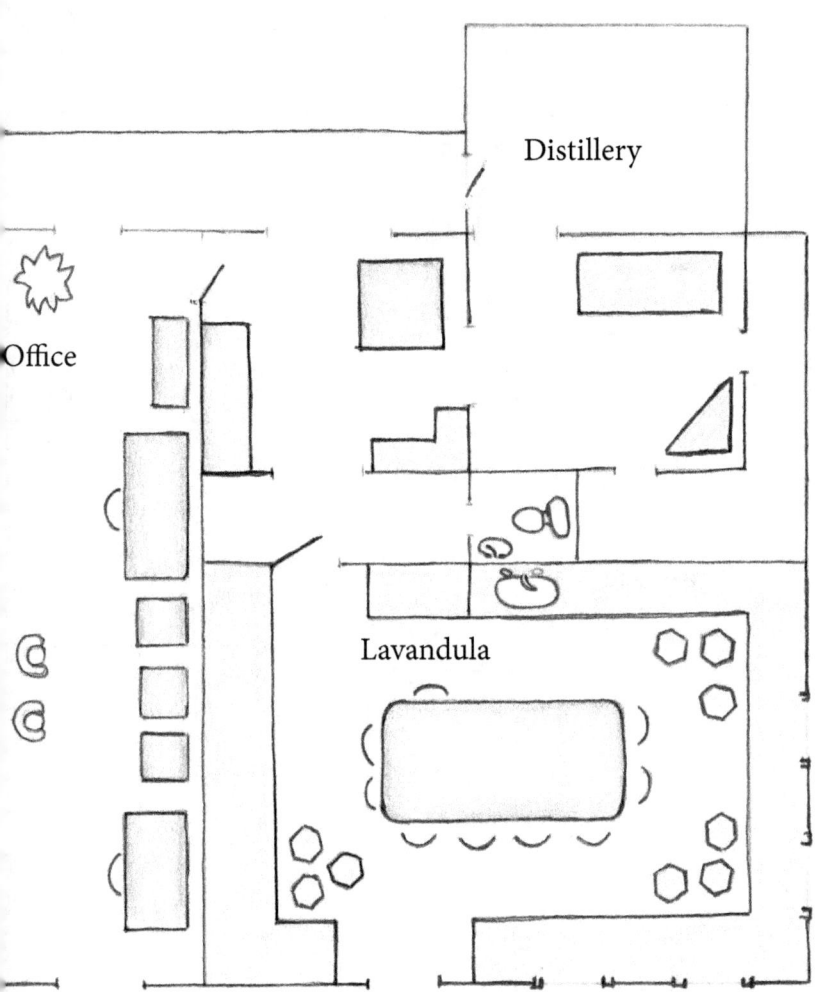

Distillery

Office

Lavandula

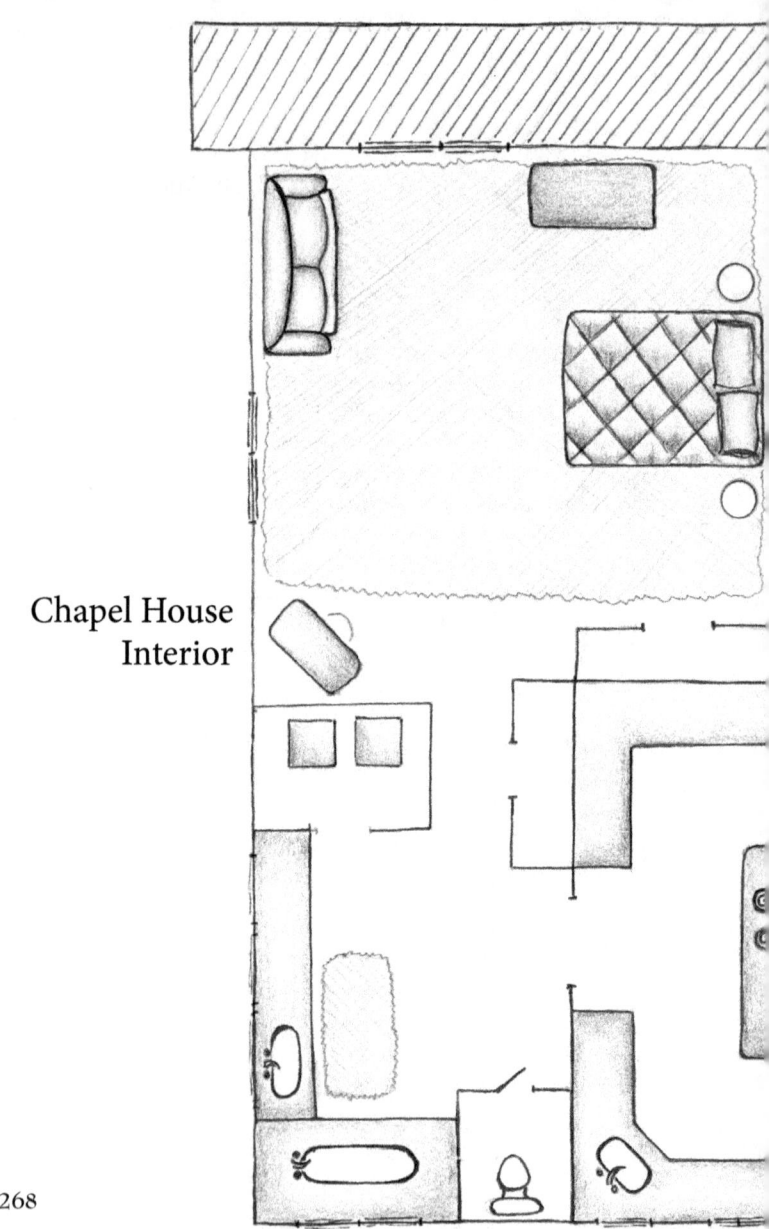

Chapel House
Interior

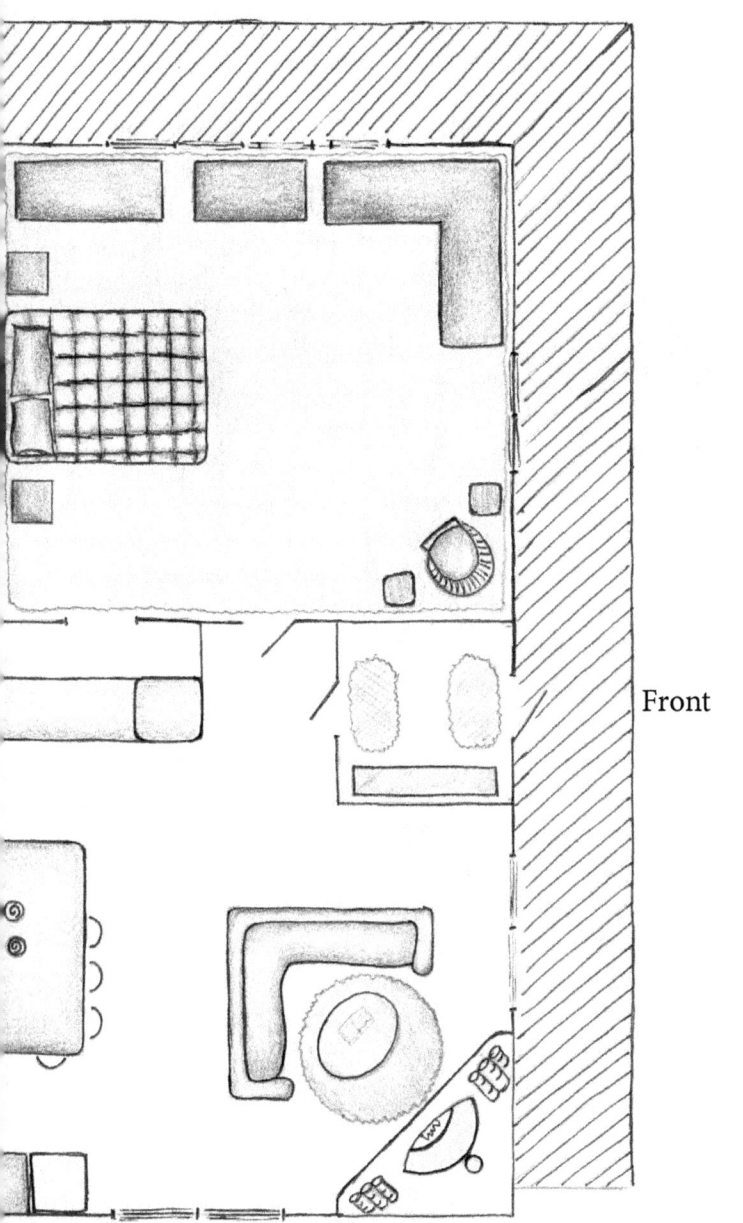

Front

269

Acknowledgements

I thank the source of all things for the sparkling gift of creativity flowing through my fingertips. Everything of interest to me is about living a beautiful life: health-affirming food, pretty and comfortable surroundings, loving relationships, words with meaning, life with spiritual growth, unconditional regard for others. I believe it is possible to make everything about creation, the created and the Creator. John Steinbeck says, "Try to understand men [people]. If you understand each other you will be kind to each other. Knowing a man [people] will never lead to hate and almost always leads to love." Everything I write is about that. Just that.

What this author needs in order to accomplish a book (other than time, discipline, a grasp of English grammar, a head full of stories and the above):

★ A pack of early readers: Nan Heflin, Frank DeLuca, Ken Gregg, Patricia Vollmer, Gate McKibbin, Katherine Edison, Dai Thomas, Gail Lindus, George Irwin, David Gordon. The comments, encouragement, especially the critiques and edits, are more valuable than prizes.

★ Another early reader, my sister-in-law Pegge Goertzen Bragg, made my favorite comment: "Sister, you have found your voice." She knows I've been looking.

★ Dai Thomas, painter of the Blue Indian Chief, Deke Harley's motorcycle, is a treasure. Her Lavandula Series tiny paintings fit my words and feelings. We are happy to have Dai on the Lucky Valley Press team.

★ John Steinbeck.

★ David Gordon. It's good to live with someone who believes in you, loves your artistic expression, your food, your nesting habits, and has your back. And he sings!

I am forever grateful to all who encourage me to tell my stories.

Love, Ginna

Deke, Interrupted
Book Two in *The Lavandula Series*
based on the fictional journals
of Stefani Michel

Book One, *Looking for John Steinbeck*
was published by Lucky Valley Press in 2016

Designed and produced by Lucky Valley Press
Jacksonville, Oregon
www.luckyvalleypress.com
Typeset in Minion, Kabel, and Bernhard Modern
All images in this book © 2017 by the artists

www.ingramcontent.com/pod-product-compliance
Lightning Source LLC
Chambersburg PA
CBHW061021120726
47910CB00006B/2046